I0532509

DEATH
IN THE SHADOWS

Book 4

The Death Card Series

By

J.S. Peck

BEJEWELED PUBLISHING
LAS VEGAS, NEVADA

Bejeweled Publishing
6480 Annie Oakley Drive
Suite 513
Las Vegas, Nevada 89120

ISBN# 978-0-9824607-8-8
First Edition: July 2020

COVER ART DESIGN: Kelly A. Martin
INTERNAL DESIGN: Jake Naylor

DEDICATION

I dedicate this book to all my readers who are learning that they are more powerful than ever when they use their awareness of what's really going on in the world of human sex trafficking and take a role to stop the perpetrators and keep the most vulnerable people safe.

Table of Contents

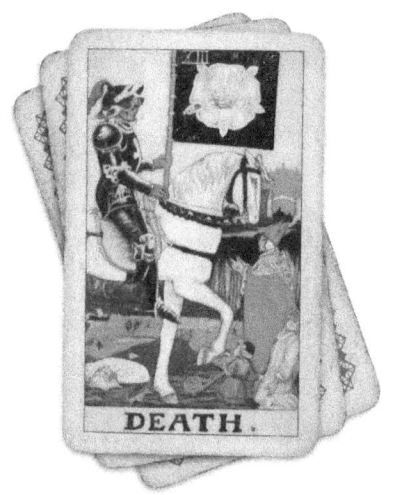

CHAPTER 1

I searched the crowd as they stood just beyond the security gate at the airport that held people back from the passengers getting off the airplane. When I saw him, our eyes locked. He smiled and lowered the dog onto the ground. Isabella and I raced forward. I flew into Mike's arms while Isabella scooped Sweet Pea up into hers.

"How was your trip?" Mike asked, holding me close.

"Short," I laughed.

As promised, Isabella and I had flown to Santa Fe for the three-day Columbus weekend so that Isabella could spend time with her Mexican family and sister-friends. Mike had stayed behind with Sweet Pea to check out an office rental space that his realtor said would soon be available. Since any rental space was often taken in a matter of hours after being offered, Mike didn't want to take a chance of losing out on it. It'd be a perfect west coast office for him and Brian to expand their successful detective agency based in Boston.

"Any luck with the rental?" I asked as we headed to the baggage area.

"Yup. Got it," Mike grinned.

"No kidding? That's great! Where's it located?"

"Right in the center of old Las Vegas near 6th Street."

"That's fabulous!" I crowed as I reached for Isabella and guided her along with us as she held Sweet Pea in her arms.

"Did you have a good time in Santa Fe, Isabella?" asked Mike.

"Yes, we're going there for Thanksgiving, too, right, Mama?"

I nodded.

"You're coming too, Mike!" Isabella said with excitement. She whispered to Sweet Pea, "And so are you!"

Sweet Pea smiled her doggy smile and wagged her tail.

Since becoming Isabella's foster mother—a role I shared with her aunt Maria in Santa Fe—Isabella had become more relaxed, not so concerned about being agreeable with everything, and no longer worried about not having me as her mother. At 11 years old, she was looking for family stability, and with Mike's and my growing relationship, things at home were pretty settled and loving. Now, if only I could say the same about the construction site where I was one of those in charge of overseeing two separate projects. That thought brought up unhappy memories.

I sighed, and Mike and Isabella looked at me, worry crossing their brows. It didn't seem possible that it'd been less than a year since Romano and I'd been in charge of overseeing the building of a restaurant and an office for the non-profit agency dealing with human trafficking. Both were on the same land that previously held the Purple Passion Lounge, where we'd worked together. So much had happened.

"Oh, it's nothing," I reassured them. "I was thinking about some loose ends that need to be cleared up."

Mike and Isabella locked eyes, and I tried to ignore them. I was excruciatingly aware that I'd escaped death several times during the last few months. First, when I'd been lovingly forced out of the way by Romano's husband while he took the full force of us being hit by a speeding car. I had a concussion and a few broken ribs, while Randy had a badly broken leg, arm, and some internal injuries, making his recovery challenging.

It was mainly because of Mike and Isabella that I'd escaped another near-death experience after I'd been kidnapped and stuffed into a drawer at the morgue. It was no wonder both looked worried since that happened only a few weeks ago. I still had aches and pains, as a reminder. I grabbed Isabella and pulled her close enough to kiss the top of her head as Mike grabbed me and did the same.

Once home, Isabella asked, "Can I run to our neighbor's house to give Gramma Irene a gift of her favorite salsa I bought for her in Santa Fe?"

"Sure, just don't take long."

Mike lifted a brow. "How long do you think she'll be? Long enough?" he asked suggestively.

"Sorry, no quickie, handsome. I love taking our time, and I don't want that to change," I whispered into Mike's ear as I pulled him close.

"Fair enough, my queen," he said before giving me a long teasing kiss that made me want to reconsider his offer.

Mike's phone rang, and he answered it, turning away. It was Brian, his business partner. Mike excitedly told him about the new rental office and pointed things out to him that the photos he'd forwarded to him hadn't shown. I watched his happy face, so glad that their west coast office was going forward and that he'd be here with Isabella and me in Las Vegas. It would've been so disappointing for all of us if that hadn't worked out.

My cell phone rang, and I was delighted to see it was Romano. "Hi, Romano. How are you and Randy making out? Is the nurse still coming every day to help him?"

"He's up every day exercising so that when his casts come off, he should be in pretty good shape."

"How's his spirit? It's not always easy to get through something like this."

"Tell me about it," he chuckled. "Yes, all is good with us. The construction site has a few issues we need to discuss, though."

"What's up there?" I asked, discouraged. "No more bones, I hope."

Two skeletons had been left on the construction site causing us issues. Although we'd identified the bones, we still hadn't found the person responsible for their murders.

"No, nothing like that, but I think the new site manager is cheating us on the construction materials."

"What happened to Butch? You mean he's no longer the site manager there?"

"Not since you left for Santa Fe. I talked to Mimi about it, and she said to schedule a meeting when you return."

"Let's meet first thing in the morning, then. How about 9 o'clock here at the house? Can you let Mimi know? I'll tell Mike."

"Sure thing. See you tomorrow."

I hung up the phone, unhappy with this new problem. Unfortunately, I didn't know enough about construction materials to ensure they met the code. But I knew someone who would know—Cal—Mike and Brian's largest client. We'd called him 'the mystery man' when we didn't realize he was the boss and not the chauffeur he portrayed. Also, he'd unwittingly become part of our family, with Isabella calling him her 'grandfather.' He looked forward to buying property here and asked me to help him. We'd made arrangements to start our search after I'd returned from Santa Fe, so now was as good a time as ever to reach out to him.

I sought out Mike. "Did you know about the situation at the construction site?"

"Mimi called me."

"Why didn't you say something?"

"I thought I'd wait until you at least had the chance to take your coat off," he teased as he pinched my cheek lovingly.

"We've set a meeting for tomorrow at 9 o'clock. I hope you can join us. I'm thinking of calling Cal. We could use his advice, don't you think?"

"Good idea. Especially with Cal's experience in construction."

"Does he know you've found a place to rent for the business?"

"Not yet. Cal will see it when we discuss his latest assignment for us—another young girl who's gone missing here in Las Vegas."

"There are so many missing young girls, aren't there?" I asked.

"Way too many. It's disturbing to realize that 5 to 6 people go missing daily here in Las Vegas. Who knew?"

"What bothers me is how many of them didn't have a choice. Human sex trafficking has become so prevalent, and it's so sad."

"All we have to do is look at Isabella to know how close she came to being a statistic in child sex trafficking," Mike added with a shake of his head. He pulled me close. "Thanks to you, that didn't happen."

"I was lucky. The right place at the right time."

"Quick thinking is more like it."

At that time, I'd escaped with four little girls who would be auctioned off. I had reacted without thinking about anything but getting them as far away as possible from what awaited them. And eventually, it ended well for all of them. Isabella was now my foster daughter, as we both wanted, and the others had made it back to their families in Mexico. I sighed, thinking about how easily some fellow humans were willing to hurt others without considering the consequences.

Home and back to problems at the construction site. It seemed as if I hadn't been away at all.

CHAPTER 2

T he following morning I stirred in bed, ready to get up. I was wired to start the day. Next to me, Mike was snoring softly, and when I looked at the clock, it was too early to get up. I thought about the girls who'd been murdered and their bones planted at the construction site. We had identified the remains as a former dancer at the Purple Passion Lounge and her roommate. They'd been killed more than five years ago, and we'd made no headway in identifying the murderer, although we thought we knew who was responsible for their deaths. When we'd searched through the files of missing young girls then, Susan and her roommate were only two of many. That was a worry.

As I stirred, Mike groaned, automatically reached out, and pulled me close to him in a spooning position. He began to nuzzle my neck, whispering sweet things into my ear, making me blush, and things went from there to a very satisfying love-making session.

Afterward, as we lay together satisfied, a knock came on the door. "C'mon in, Isabella," I called out.

Already in her school uniform, Isabella and Sweet Pea jumped up on the bed as they usually did most mornings. She asked, "Do you think it'd be okay to take salsa to the two headmistresses?"

"I think that'd be a great idea. After all, who doesn't love good salsa from Santa Fe?"

"You're so funny, Mama."

"Who wants some of my famous scrambled eggs?" asked Mike.

"I do," Isabella and I chorused.

"Then get up, my queen, and get dressed. Want to fix the toast, Isabella?"

"Yes, I do!"

I smiled as I watched them head downstairs, feeling so blessed to have them in my life. I wanted to make sure that nothing happened to either one of them. Lately, it seemed that there had been so much trouble surrounding us. It would be nice to escape to Santa Fe for Thanksgiving, this time with Mike and Sweet Pea. A few days ago, I'd had just a quick moment to say hello to Coyote in Santa Fe, the sheriff there, before we returned to Las Vegas. I knew he wanted to see if my psychic abilities could answer some of his questions about human trafficking there. I'd promised Coyote that Mike and I would sit with him at Thanksgiving time to review some of his files and see how we could help him.

Isabella was so excited about returning to school that I could barely grab and kiss her goodbye before she raced out the door and ran to the school bus driving her to the private Wilson Charter School. She loved going to school and was doing well in her 5th-grade class. The only problem occurred when a taller girl tried to bully her. But that had ended quickly enough when Isabella had pushed her down and made her cry. Strangely, that incident had made them odd friends of sorts.

Virginia arrived soon after Isabella left for school, and I was happy to see her. She was quickly becoming more than a housekeeper and a babysitter for us, and I was glad we were becoming closer as friends. We chatted while I pulled cookies from the freezer I'd serve at the meeting. When I began to fix the coffee, my cell phone rang.

"Virginia, since my hands are wet, can you please pick up my phone from the counter and answer it? Tell whoever it is to please hold, and I'll be with them in a second."

Virginia's face turned pink when she saw who it was.

"Hello, Cal. No, this is Virginia. I'm answering the phone for her while she dries her hands." Pause. "I'm good, thank you. I hear you're heading our way soon. That'll be nice. Thanks, I will. You, too. Here she is," she added, holding the phone out for me to take and flapping her hands in front of her as if she were hot.

Oh, my! I didn't realize there was a possibility she'd be interested in him. That could be a lot of fun, I thought.

"Hi, Cal. When do you think you'll head our way? Remember, you've got a room right here, and Isabella will be disappointed if you don't stay with us. We'd all love to see you," I said, emphasizing the all. "Good, we'll see you the day after tomorrow, then. Drive safely, okay?"

After I hung up, I teased, "Do you have something you want to tell me, Virginia?"

She looked mortified but then smiled. "Cal's such a nice person, isn't he?"

"Yes, and I'm glad you think so too."

"You are?" Virginia asked.

I put my arm around her. "Yes, I am."

The doorbell rang, and Mike beat me to it. "C'mon in, everybody."

I was ecstatic to see Mimi and Romano again, and we greeted each other with hugs and kisses. "Let's go into the dining room. I have coffee and cookies waiting for us."

Upon hearing the word cookies, Romano patted his stomach and pulled out his pants at his waistline. "See? I've lost a lot of weight, haven't I? That means I can have two cookies," he said hopefully.

Mike, Mimi, and I eyed each other and burst out laughing.

After we grabbed a coffee and sat down, Mike said, "Rosie and I haven't talked about what's going on at the construction site, so Romano, why'd don't you fill her in on what makes you think the materials are deficient and not part of the contract?"

"Late Saturday afternoon, I stopped at the site. Plywood and studs were unloaded, and those delivered earlier were re-loaded onto the truck. When I asked the new site manager what he was doing, he told me to get the f... out of the way. He said the order they'd received earlier was wrong, and the driver was there to take it back. But the new materials didn't look as nice."

When we smiled, he said, "You know what I mean."

"And why were they there so late in the day?" I asked.

Romano said, "Your guess is as good as mine. Maybe so the day crew wouldn't question the exchange?"

Mike pushed the stack of papers that he'd brought to the table forward. "I've looked through the contract as you wanted me to, Mimi. It clearly states that the material used would be above standard. For example, the contractor will use 2x6″ studs instead of 2x4″ studs, and the plywood would be ¾″ and not ½″ and so on."

"That's right. My father distinctly had me put that into the contract," added Mimi. "I guess he knew what could happen."

"Before we head down there, I think it'd be good to stop at the building supply company and get a copy of the invoices for the delivered items. They should have left copies at the construction site, but I want to see what the company has on file. Mimi, you should come with me if they wonder who I am asking for the invoices."

"Aw, right. That's a good idea."

"Rosie? Did you get hold of Cal?" asked Mike.

"I did, and he's going to be here tomorrow."

"Good. Cal is experienced in construction work, and he'll be a good one to talk to us about what to look for regarding the materials and the cost estimates."

"Is this always happening on the larger construction jobs around town?" I asked.

"Everyone's watching their bottom line, and sometimes it's easy to pull the wool over anyone's eyes if they're not double-checking everything. Remember, there's always greed, and this is no small job that you all are vested in, especially since none of you have experience in contractor work," Mike said.

Miserable, we nodded.

"Mimi, although you've hired a local accountant here to handle the accounting of the expenses, it's up to all three of you to make sure the figures you turn in are correct."

Unhappy, we looked at each other, hating that we should have been more on the ball. Maybe we were in over our heads with this, I thought.

11

But Mimi was having none of it. "Look, don't be discouraged, we'll get this straightened out, and then we'll set up daily meetings with the new site manager going forward. We can take turns doing that."

Both Romano and I perked up at hearing this.

"Who is this new dude, Mimi?" asked Romano.

"Red Scarvoni. He's taking Butch's place. I will check in with my father to see if he knows anything about him or his family."

"Good idea," Mike agreed as he rose to answer his phone.

"Did I miss anything else while I was away? Any news regarding who murdered the girls?" I asked.

Romano and Mimi shook their heads. "Nothing yet."

"This next part of the construction will fly along now, so we'll need to watch every move," said Mimi.

We nodded in agreement.

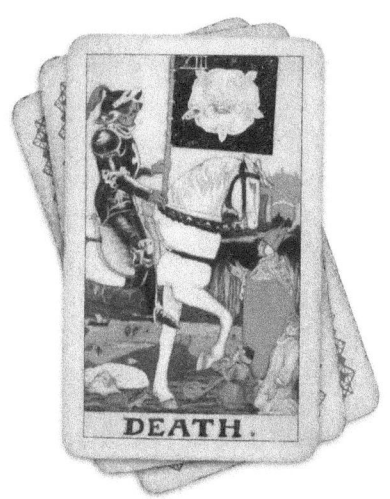

CHAPTER 3

S omething was up. When Isabella returned home, she was quiet and not her enthusiastic self. I knew if I waited long enough, she'd come to me and talk about whatever was bothering her.

Isabella was pretty savvy and certainly had gained a lot of "street smarts" living in Mexico with her parents and siblings. Her father was abusive, and her mother had sold Isabella to become a domestic to save her from how they were living in Mexico. She wanted Isabella to have a better life in America—not realizing she'd signed her daughter into a sex trafficking scheme. Despite what she'd endured so far, Isabella was a wise old soul with an understanding of life that was unusual for her age. She just needed time to figure things out on her own.

I began to look through the MLM property listings to see what was for sale in the Henderson part of the

Las Vegas valley. It was fascinating to discover so many charming small housing complexes and neighborhoods tucked away in the Las Vegas area. Vegas hadn't become property zoned and planned out until much later in the 1990s and 2000s. So behind shopping malls and other industries were surprisingly beautiful neighborhoods and smaller housing complexes you'd never know were there. Vegas was a surprise for many reasons, but housing was one for sure.

I saw a large house for sale not far from us that had great potential. It even had a small guest house on the property. Immediately, it came to my mind that it'd be an excellent place for Virginia to rent. I chuckled to myself. I'd never played matchmaker before, but it could be fun. However, I'd keep that to myself at the moment.

My cell phone rang, and I answered without checking who was calling. "Hello?"

My heart dropped as soon as I recognized the voice. It was my dead fiancé's police partner, Jerry. "Haven't figured it out yet, have you?" he asked, slurring his words. He sounded very drunk.

"What are you talking about?" I asked, already knowing what he meant.

"You want to know who murdered those girls, don't you? Want to know if there were more than those two?" I gasped, and he laughed. "Pay me enough money, and maybe I'll tell you."

I flared angrily at the thought that everything boiled down to money; how I hated that! "I already know who killed those girls," I stated with authority. "So, no, thank you, not interested," I lied.

His laughter died, and he whined, "You're not even interested in where they're buried?" he asked, sounding deflated.

"Nope," I answered. "You already told me, but you probably don't remember it because you were so drunk," I lied again.

"I don't think so, lady. I never told you that," he challenged.

"The desert is a great place to bury bodies. The problem is remembering where. Isn't that right, Jerry? And you don't remember, do you?"

"I do so. Just because the creek dried up doesn't mean I can't find the place again."

I perked up at that. I'd learned something new—a creek was involved. I needed to know more. "You mean that old creek off Route 15?"

"No, you don't. I'm not saying another word without you paying me money." He hung up before I could respond.

I tried calling him back, but he didn't answer, and I decided not to leave a message. I didn't want him to think I was desperate. My hands began to shake with anger. The audacity of that man to call and expect me to give in to his demand for money! He'd been right about my wanting to know who'd murdered the girls, though. I'd give almost anything to learn who'd been the one to kill those girls whose bones had been dumped at the construction site. I was pretty sure it'd been the former Chief of Police who had ordered their deaths, but I didn't know who had made the actual killing.

It still pained me to know that it'd been the police chief who had ordered the death of my fiancé when he'd refused to be involved in the drugs being sold by those from the chief's precinct. Now that the police chief was dead, I couldn't do more than grumble about it.

I called Mike to let him know what'd happened, but he didn't answer. I left a message for him to call me back. I sat at the kitchen table and held my head in my hands. I leaned forward and closed my eyes. As a psychic, I could sometimes get visions if I concentrated hard enough. I tried to picture a running creek in the desert that was now dry. A flash came to me of an area I'd seen as a kid when our science class had gone out to the desert to study the fauna that grew in our climate. There were beautiful small colored flowers on plants that ran in bunches alongside a small creek area. I could still envision their vibrant purple color.

I remembered the trip well because it was one of the only times I'd been on a school outing where the boys in the class hadn't teased or bullied me. Where had we gone that day? It couldn't have been that far into the desert, yet I remembered it had taken some time for the bus to get us there. I envisioned that trip from when I loaded onto the bus until we arrived. If my memory was correct, it was about a 45 to 60-minute drive from town. I knew I'd want to search that area—something to do in my spare time.

Isabella entered the kitchen and plopped down in the chair across from me, holding Sweet Pea in her arms.

"Mama?"

"What, sweetheart?"

"I thought I'd invite Tiffany to ride home with me after school tomorrow if that's okay with you."

"She's in the 6th grade, a class ahead of you, right?"

"Yes, but we're in the same art class."

"I didn't realize that you've become close friends, Isabella. What changed your mind?"

"Well, I feel sorry for her. Nobody likes her. They're afraid of her because she's bigger and stronger than most kids there."

"Hmm. That's an interesting thought. Isn't Tiffany nearly two years older than you?"

"Mama, I think she needs a friend."

"Well, I guess the question then becomes, do you want the same thing—to be friends with her?"

Isabella looked down, lost in thought. "What is it, Isabella?"

"Mama, she asked if she could come home with me. I said I'd have to ask you first."

"Are you sure you want to do this? You have a choice, you know."

"I know."

"Here's the deal then. Before anyone of your friends can come to the house after school, I need an okay from their parents. So tell Tiffany to give you her home telephone number so I can ask her parents for permission to have her here."

"Okay, I'll call her right now. I have her cell phone number."

I watched Isabella walk away to get the phone she'd left upstairs. I wasn't entirely comfortable with Tiffany as a friend for Isabella since she'd been the one to knock her down on the first day of school. She'd never said she was sorry or had helped Isabella pick up the books she'd knocked out of her hands. I sighed. I knew I could be somewhat overprotective of Isabella, so maybe it was time I relaxed and let Isabella try their relationship.

When I called Tiffany's mother, it sounded like she was occupied with something else and uninterested in speaking with me. "So then," I finished, "is it okay with you if Tiffany comes to our house after school and stays for dinner? We'll drive her home around 8 o'clock?"

"Don't bother to drive her home. Have Tiffany call here, and the chauffeur will pick her up."

"Well, here's our telephone number in case something comes up."

"That's not necessary. If Tiffany needs anything, she can call."

"It was nice speaking to you …"

"Yeah, you too. Sorry, I've got to run."

I hung up the phone with my mouth hanging open. I drew a deep breath and knew trouble was brewing with our having anything to do with Tiffany and her family. I felt sorry for Tiffany because she seemed to be on her own. No wonder she wanted to find a place to go after school other than her home, I thought, unfairly.

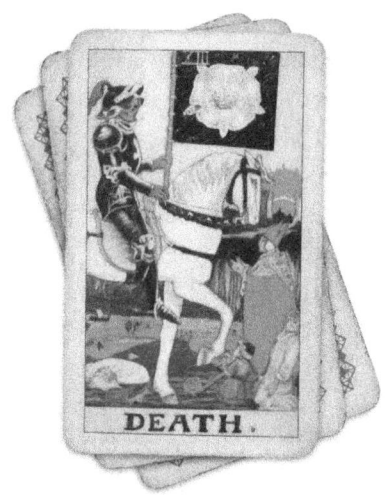

CHAPTER 4

W hen Mike got home, he came and pulled me into his arms. His eyes twinkled, and he was excited about the new office space. "Tomorrow, after Isabella leaves for school, I thought we'd ride to some furniture stores to look for desks, chairs, couches, and stuff for the new office."

"Sure, that sounds nice," I answered quietly.

"What's wrong, Rosie?" he asked, tipping my head up and looking deep into my eyes. He put his arm around me and walked me over to the couch. "Sit down and tell me."

I told him about my conversation with Tiffany's mother, who didn't seem to care where her daughter went after school—as long as it didn't cut into her plans.

Mike shook his head. His eyes hardened. "I can relate," he said. "It's not easy being a kid left on your own."

That was one of the few times Mike had referred to his childhood, and I felt his sorrow. I leaned forward, put my arm around his shoulder, and kissed him thoroughly on the lips. "I love you, Mike."

He returned the kiss with ardor. "I love you too, Rosie." He searched my eyes. "What else is bothering you? I can tell you've something more to say."

I was amazed at how quickly Mike had become attuned to me and familiar with my thoughts and emotions. I told him about my call from Jerry, and he immediately began setting boundaries for me, which I hated him doing. It was something we argued about from time to time. I not only didn't like to be restricted from doing what I wanted to do—within reason—but I firmly believed that I didn't need his approval for anything I felt was necessary for me to do.

"Before you go trotting off and getting yourself in trouble, we must make a plan. Did you let the police chief know about the call? I can't imagine Roberto will be happy to hear of this."

"No, I wanted to run this by you first. I have to say that I was surprised Jerry called because I thought he was still in jail."

"Since he's not accused of murder, only withholding evidence, I'm sure he's out on bail and won't be going before the judge for a while."

"What should I do if he calls again?"

"We'll have to talk to Roberto about that. But I think you should push the record button on your phone as soon as possible so you can record every word he says. You downloaded the Tape a Call apt like I asked you to do, didn't you?"

"Yes, I did."

"Jerry asking to be paid for information only puts him in a worse bind legally. It proves he knows much more about what happened back then than he's willing to admit."

I nodded in agreement.

Mike cleared his throat. "Now, as far as you going out to the desert on your own, that's not going to happen," he stated firmly.

I felt my face grow hot. I hated it when Mike tried to tell me what I could or could not do. However, I held back a snippy reply. "Then you'll have to make time to go with me. Agreed? Or maybe Cal can join me."

"Do you think you know where Jerry is talking about?"

"I know it's been a while, but I remember a school trip so vividly that I think I might find the spot... eventually."

Mike tipped his head back and forth as if to say maybe.

To change the subject, I asked, "How are you coming with finding the young girl missing here in Vegas?"

"I spent time with Roberto this morning. I'm glad he's allowed me to use their empty office, but I'll happily have my office space. To answer your question—I'm stuck for the moment. We'll always be looking for someone since so many girls have gone missing here."

I had to agree. Ever since I'd read the tarot cards for Melissa, I had come to see Vegas in a different light. By being exposed to her murder and its harshness, I'd been pushed out of my comfort of the more loving, spiritual way of living and had become somewhat hardened.

Sweet Pea came running down the stairs and stood at my feet. She barked and then headed to the sliding door in the kitchen. I opened the door to let her out and watched her go to the side of the house, which was her private area.

Watching Sweet Pea, I was reminded that my sister-friends had given her to me as a gift after Jeff's murder. It seemed impossible that more than three years had passed already. So much had happened. I was in such a good spot in my life now. Isabella and Mike were here with me, and I had new friends that meant the world to me—Romano, Randy, and Mimi. I had a new family in Santa Fe—Maria, Miguel, Angela, Armando, Ricardo, little Miguel, and Rosa. And, of course, I still had my besties— my sister-friends—Karen, Susannah, and Nancy. And to think of all the lonely, sad tears I'd shed while alone after Jeff's death. My eyes watered as I thought of how blessed I was.

Isabella had followed Sweet Pea down and stood by me. She leaned into me, and I kissed the top of her head. Then Isabella wrapped her arms around me; it was a special moment. She looked up at me and smiled. "What's for supper, Mama?"

I laughed, back to the reality of having a hungry kid waiting for dinner.

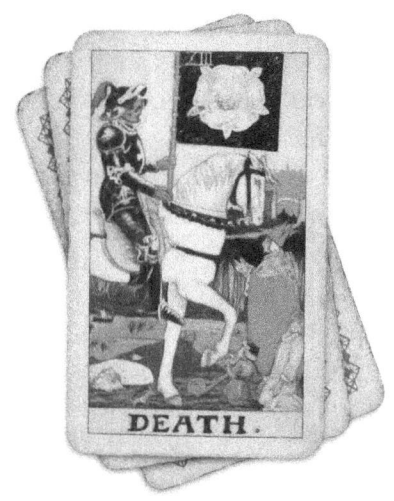

CHAPTER 5

I woke up excited that Cal would be arriving later. I went downstairs and fixed the coffee while Mike took a shower. When Isabella entered the kitchen, she asked, "Is Grandfather coming today?"

I smiled. Isabella had taken to Cal, calling him Grandfather in the same honoring manner she had referred to the old Indian woman in Santa Fe as Grandmother. That same Grandmother of today had been our mother in the past, and I had been Isabella's sister. Past lives were so fascinating how they could become entwined in modern times.

"Yes, he is. Did you pick up your mess in the bathroom?"

Her expression said it all. "I'll go back up after I eat, okay?"

I nodded. "Have you planned what you and Tiffany will do after school?"

"Is Mike going to grill hamburgers tonight?"

"He can if that's what you'd like for supper."

"I thought we could make brownies for dessert then. Does that sound okay?"

"Sure, you can use a mix in the cupboard."

"Yes!" she said, making the victory motion of a pumped fist. Something learned at school, no doubt. I knew Isabella was working hard to fit in at school; this was just one example she used.

After Isabella left for the school bus, Mike turned to me. "Ready? Shall we go shopping for the new office?"

"As long as I'm back at 3 o'clock at the latest. Cal said he should be here by then."

"Isn't Virginia coming today? She'll be here to let him in."

At my pleased expression of envisioning them together, Mike said, "What? What's going on?"

"Nothing," I smiled. "I'll get my purse."

If we looked at one couch or one desk, we looked at 20. We sat in various spots on each sofa and tried out each desk chair to test them. We bought the same desk for Mike's office and the spare office with different small leather couches and stuffed chairs for guests. We chose several artwork pieces to give each office a slightly different feel and look. In the front area, we decided on a smaller, more feminine desk and a suede leather L-shape couch for clients and prospective clients to sit on that would take up the entire area opposite the desk. I was pleased, though tired, with what we'd chosen. I smiled at Mike, looking all done in. Shopping wasn't his bag—pun intended.

We arrived home just before 3 o'clock and saw Cal's car in the driveway. Entering the house, we heard laughter and headed into the kitchen to see Cal and Virginia sitting at the table sipping tea. Virginia's pink cheeks gave away her pleasure, and when Cal turned to greet us, his cheeks were as pink as hers. His eyes sparkled, and my heart lifted. It was beautiful to see both of them so happy. Virginia rose and fixed Mike and me a cup of tea, and we joined them at the table.

As we finished our drinks, Isabella and Tiffany came through the door. As soon as Isabella saw Cal, she ran forward. "Hi, Grandfather!"

He opened his arms wide. "C'mon here, Isabella, so that I can give you a big hug."

Once he released her, Isabella turned to Tiffany. "This is Grandfather, Virginia, Mama, and Mike," she announced as she had been taught to do.

Instead of shaking hands or greeting us, Tiffany stood there silent. "I'm hungry. Do you have anything to eat?"

"Sure. Do you want a banana?" Isabella blushed at Tiffany's rudeness.

"I guess."

All four of us sat there, not knowing what to say to a young girl with no manners. Sweet Pea scurried out from beneath the table where she had been resting and went to Isabella for a quick pat on the head. She completely ignored Tiffany, who had no interest in her. That in itself was unusual.

"Why don't you sit here while I get you something to drink? You must be thirsty after a long day at school." I handed them each a cold water bottle, making Tiffany scowl.

"Don't you have any soda?" Tiffany asked, surprised.

"No. Mama doesn't allow it. Too much sugar," answered Isabella.

"That's too bad. I can have whatever I want at my house," Tiffany stated.

Everything but love, I thought, unfairly. After I got out the package of brownie mix from the cupboard, I told Isabella, "I'm going to be in my office with Mike and Grandfather. If you need anything, come get me."

"Okay, Mama."

As I walked away, I heard Tiffany ask, "You mean you have to do all the cooking here?"

I shook my head in wonder at her misconception. Isabella was going to have her hands' full dealing with Tiffany.

Mike and I had asked Cal to meet us in the office so we could fill him in on what'd been happening. Cal had become wealthy when he'd invented several items—one of which had something to do with construction—making him familiar with job sites, estimates, and knowledge of building materials.

"Yup, I'm happy to go over everything for you at the construction site," he said.

Then I told him about Jerry's call and his asking for money for information about the murdered girls and whether there were more bones to be found. When I told him that I thought I might be able to locate the site, he got excited.

"Yeah. I'll happily go with you to search for the place."

Mike looked pleased. It was easy to read his mind that between Cal and himself, I wouldn't be apt to wander into the desert by myself. That was fine with me.

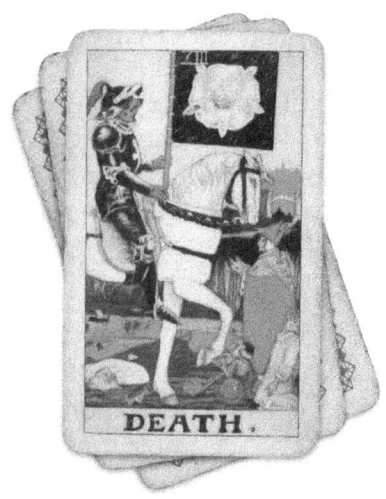

CHAPTER 6

I asked Virginia to join us for dinner, and she and Cal seemed pleased that I had. While Virginia set the table, I made the salad. Mike was outside grilling the hamburgers while Isabella and Tiffany stood watching him. I heard Tiffany say, "Don't you have any hotdogs?"

I bent my ear toward the sliding glass door to hear his response. "Nope. Tonight it's hamburgers."

"Oh," Tiffany replied.

I smiled to myself. Mike's tone of voice left no room for debate. I'd have to practice that same one. I felt it would be needed if we were involved with Tiffany.

After dinner, Isabella carried in the brownies she and Tiffany had cut and laid onto a beautiful antique plate. When Cal saw this, he exclaimed, "Oh my! Did you girls bake these yourselves?"

Before Isabella could say anything, Tiffany said, "I baked them."

"Well, Isabella and Tiffany, they look mighty fine. Thank you both for making them for dessert," Cal said, determined not to leave Isabella out.

Tiffany's face lit up with pleasure, and I thought to ask. "Is this the first time you've baked brownies, Tiffany?"

"Uh-huh."

"Isabella knows how to make a cake with icing too. Maybe you'd like to try that next time."

Tiffany studied me as if to question whether there'd be a next time. I smiled and said nothing.

After dinner, the girls went to Isabella's bedroom to study. Virginia and I cleaned up while Mike and Cal went outside for a nightcap on the patio. Then, Virginia went to say goodnight to them while I fixed myself a nightcap and went to join them.

It felt good to be outside, where it was cooler and refreshing. "Well, Mike, what do you think about Tiffany?" I asked.

He locked eyes with Cal. "We were just talking about her. She's going to be someone to keep an eye on, for sure. I hope Isabella knows that as well."

"We'll have to talk to her about it. She seems determined to be a friend to Tiffany, saying that she isn't well-liked and needs a friend."

"Tiffany is quite a bit older and more physically developed. We're both more concerned for Isabella's well-being, that's all."

I nodded in agreement. "Me, too." I turned to Cal, "Well, Cal, it seems you and Virginia are getting along just fine. She's nice, isn't she?"

"She's a peach, all right. So, when do you want me to look at that house you mentioned?"

"We have an appointment tomorrow at 10 o'clock to see it. Does that work for you?"

"Sounds good to me."

Mike looked at his watch. "What time are you supposed to drive Tiffany home?"

"What time is it now?"

"7:30," Mike answered.

"In about 15 minutes, I'll have her call her chauffeur. That's what her mother wants her to do. Can you imagine?"

Mike and Cal shook their heads, and I went inside to set things in motion.

After Tiffany left, I sat with Isabella. "Did you have a good time having Tiffany here?"

"It was okay, Mama."

"Mike, Grandfather, and I want to make sure that you know that friendships only work when both people involved in the relationship are happy to be together. Although you feel sorry for Tiffany, that's not a good enough reason to become her friend. On the other hand, friendships usually take time to develop. So let's give it some time, and then you can decide. Does that sound like a plan?"

"Yes, Mama." She reached for my hand. "I don't think Tiffany has a real family as I do. She said that she usually eats alone."

"That's pretty sad, isn't it?"

Isabella nodded. I leaned down and kissed her on each cheek. "I'm so happy we're a family now. I love you, Isabella."

"I love you always, Mama."

There it was again. That somewhat different way of expressing herself—a blessing of sorts—and I felt a peace that only comes from having a child in your life that you love with all your heart.

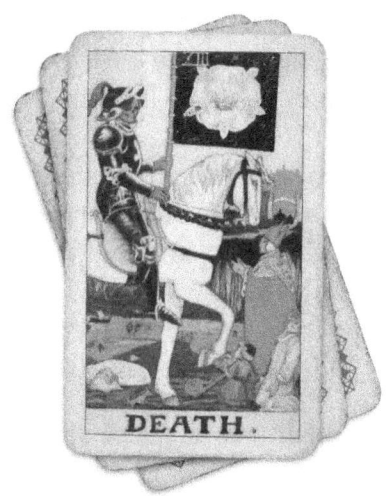

CHAPTER 7

I awoke early the following day and felt Mike's arm around me as he pulled me against him. In a husky voice, he whispered into my ear, "Good morning, my queen." Then he turned me toward him, pushed my hair behind my ear, and looked at me with such love that I could barely breathe. "Let me show you how much I love you. Are you okay with that?" he asked with smoldering eyes.

He had his answer as I reached for his hand and placed it against me.

After our lovemaking, Mike held me close and sighed. "I don't think I'll ever tire of loving you."

"I'm counting on that," I chuckled as I pulled him closer and kissed him before I got up to shower.

When I stepped out of the shower, I hurriedly dressed and went downstairs, greeted by the smell of coffee brewing and bacon cooking. When I entered the kitchen, Mike handed me a cup of coffee and gave one to Cal, who had come behind me. Where's Isabella?" Cal asked as he searched the room.

"Here I am!" came a sweet, excited voice as Isabella raced into the room with Sweet Pea at her heels.

Cal set down his coffee and held his arms wide for Isabella to nestle in while Sweet Pea barked and jumped up and down, wanting the same attention. We laughed at her antics until I called for her. "Time to go out, Sweet Pea. Come on!"

I hurriedly turned away from the sight of Isabella and Cal together because it brought tears to my eyes. They had formed their relationship partly because each needed a loving family and was glad the other was now a part of it.

After Isabella left for school, Mike went to receive the new furniture at his office downtown, and Cal and I went into the office, where I laid out a map of the broader area surrounding Las Vegas. It wasn't detailed and not helpful, so we turned to the computer to see what we could download. We had luck when we went to the US Forest Service website, used their interactive map system, and found the Tule Springs Fossil Beds area north of North Las Vegas. Unsurprisingly, the map showed no dried-up creek, but I printed out the plan anyway. When I took my school trip, I remembered something about fossils being nearby, but we had not visited the site.

Cal looked thoughtful. "Are you sure this is the spot?"

"No," I answered honestly. "I won't know until I get there." I rose from my chair. "Ready to go and see your new house?" I teased.

"Oh, you think so, do you?"

I just smiled. I'd already had a vision of Cal living there.

"Do you have a tape measure? And we'll need to bring paper and pen to make notes," Cal asked with a lilt in his voice.

We loaded into my SUV and took off. I turned down a quiet street near my house where an older community of charming larger homes was tucked away amid their well-kept landscapes. The place we wanted to view was the largest one at the end of the cul-de-sac, where I could barely make out the small guest house set back from the road. It reminded me of the carriage houses back east remodeled as separate dwellings. I thought the guest house might work out for Virginia since she'd told me she would look for another place to rent when her lease ran out.

A snazzy-looking red convertible sat in the driveway that I was sure belonged to the real estate agent. Sure enough, Sylvia stepped out and greeted us as we pulled in behind her car and parked.

"Howdy, Rosie. And this must be Cal. Glad to meet you, Cal. I'm Sylvia Brooks, your real estate agent."

"Yes, it's nice to meet you too," he said as he shook her hand.

"It's a pretty house, isn't it? It just came on the market, so we're the first to see it. Let's go on in, shall we?"

We followed her up the walk and into the courtyard before the house. It was breathtaking with its beautiful plants and cacti scattered among small round stones and alongside the Mexican tiles used as a pathway. "Beautiful," I remarked.

"Wait until you see the inside of the house. They did a lovely job of decorating. You won't have to change a thing."

Cal put an arm on my shoulder fatherly, and we followed Sylvia inside. The foyer was large, two stories high, with a skylight lighting the room. Beautiful marble tile was on the floor, and a fireplace was set into the wall. We followed Sylvia around the first floor and then upstairs to see the large master bedroom suite and three other bedrooms. I looked at Cal, who seemed pleased. How the house was laid out didn't look overpowering or seem too much for Cal to handle alone. I was sure he'd have help to care for it anyway.

I'd change a few things about the house if it were mine. The kitchen cabinets were dark and not that attractive. I'd paint them a lighter shade or two than the color of the wall. I noticed Cal checking out the water filter system underneath the kitchen sink and writing something down. Then, he wandered back through the house and looked at the mechanical workings of the place, jotting down more notes on his pad.

When we went outside, Sylvia chuckled at our expressions. The outside was stunning, with a large patio and a small but beautiful pool and Jacuzzi. The plantings all around the yard were gorgeous. I didn't think I'd ever seen a prettier backyard. I could envision Isabella in the pool with her friends. I hoped Cal would be up for that. I looked to Cal, who smiled back at me, pleased.

An hour later, we finished the tour. We arranged with Sylvia to return at 5 o'clock to show the house to Mike and Isabella. We'd also ask Virginia to join us since she'd be at home waiting for Isabella after school. I'd requested Virginia to be there then so Cal and I could review the lumber company invoices with Romano and Mimi. We were meeting at Mimi's condo that she was renting just off the strip. Mike would join us if he could make it.

"Well, Cal, what did you think about the house?"

"The bones are good, and the mechanicals look in pretty good shape. I want to check out the air conditioner, though, since it looks old. The little house in the back could be a problem, though."

"Why?" I asked, perplexed.

"An empty place like that invites trouble."

"Why not rent it out?"

"I'm a pretty private person. I wouldn't want just anyone living there."

"I don't blame you. I have someone in mind that would be perfect to live there," I added excitedly.

Cal cocked a brow at me. "Oh?"

"My friend will be looking for a new place to rent when her release comes due. She'd be perfect," I added with a grin.

"I don't know. I can't even think about it right now."

"Don't you even want to know who it is?"

He laughed. "You're going to tell me anyhow, aren't you?"

"Virginia," I said, watching his expression.

"Virginia? Really?" His eyes lit up.

"Yup. She'd be the perfect person to rent it. She could keep an eye on the place when you're not there too."

He nodded. "Yeah, that might work."

"I haven't said a word to her about this idea. But let's see what she says after she sees the place tonight, okay?"

"Okay, by me," he said, a lilt in his voice.

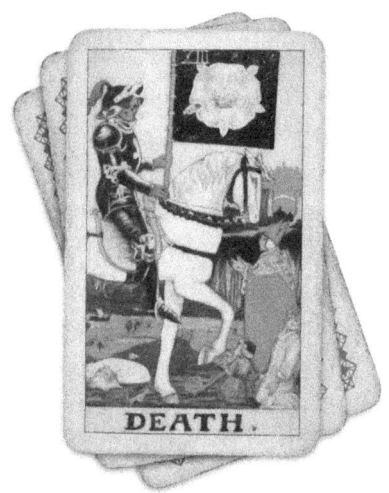

CHAPTER 8

When we walked through the door of Mimi's condo, something smelled divine, and I groaned with pleasure. "Mimi, what are you cooking?" I asked as I hugged her in greeting.

"Romano brought us an apple pie to bake." Patting her rounded tummy, she smiled. "I've been missing his sweets."

"Me too," I answered. "Where's Romano?"

"He's waiting for us in the dining room."

Romano rose to greet us as soon as he saw us, beaming. He hugged me with enthusiasm and then shook Cal's hand. "I'm glad you're here, Cal."

"What are you all smiles about, Romano?" I asked.

"Randy has a new walking cast and can finally move around independently. We want to invite you all for dinner tomorrow night. It'll be the first time in a long time that he'll be able to join us."

"That's fabulous. A true cause for celebration!"

He nodded. "How does 7 o'clock sound? And please, don't bring anything; I've got it covered."

While munching on sandwiches and waiting for the pie to cool, we took turns looking through the slips. Mimi had put them in order, separating them into two piles. The first pile consisted of copies of the delivery slips left on-site, and the other pile consisted of photocopies of the invoices that the lumber company was charging for the items. Not all of the things matched to what had been delivered and charged. I felt goosebumps as I felt my grandmother's energy around me. Was she warning us to be careful?

"Cal? When you look at the items left at the job site, you'll see that some were not checked off and initialed by whoever received them as they were supposed to. So, the only way to prove the difference is to compare the installed items to what the invoices say was left, right? Are you willing to do that?"

"I'm glad to help, Mimi."

"I think the real question is, what can we do about the installed materials not part of the quote?" I asked.

"Have you talked to the owner of the construction company, Mimi?" asked Cal.

"No, I wanted to see where we stood first."

"Why don't you call him right now and ask him to meet us first thing tomorrow at the site? Tell him it's an emergency. If he gives you any trouble, tell him you will halt construction until he has time to meet with us."

Mimi's educational background in business made her knowledgeable about how things worked in the corporate world, yet, her upbringing in a mafia family made her challenging when needed. When she rejoined us after the call, she wore a satisfied expression. "We're meeting at 7:30 tomorrow morning before the crew starts at 8."

"Where's Butch in all this?" I asked. "Isn't he supposed to be the foreman on this job?"

"Who knows? When I asked Red where he was, he said he didn't know," answered Romano.

"Are Tony and Lorenzo still in town, Mimi? Maybe Tony knows something since he acted like he and Butch were great friends when I saw them on the construction site a few weeks back," I added.

"I haven't talked to him, but as far as I know, my cousin and his flunky, Lorenzo, are still here. Since they were responsible for the car accident that hurt you and Randy, they must stay in town until Randy is completely healed and they are cleared of vehicle homicide."

My cell phone buzzed. It was a text message from Isabella asking when I'd be home. I looked at the time displayed on my phone. "I can't believe it's four o'clock already. Where did the time go? We better get on home, Cal."

We all rose to gather our things and head out. "See you tomorrow at 7:30, everyone," said Mimi as she closed the door behind us.

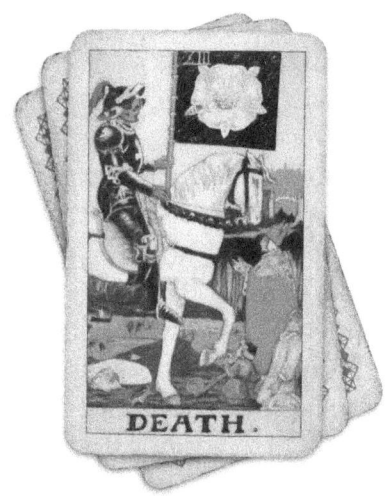

CHAPTER 9

M ike pulled into the driveway at the same time we did. I'd texted him earlier about our appointment to see the house and to ensure he got home in time for the viewing. I went to him as he climbed out of the car. "Hi there, handsome. I'm glad you made it home in time."

He kissed me enthusiastically. "I wouldn't miss it."

When we got inside, both Isabella and Sweet Pea came running. "Hi, Grandfather. Want to see what I wrote in school today?"

"Yes, I do. Let's sit at the table, and you can show me."

"Hi, Virginia." I greeted her. "Cal is looking to buy a house not far from here. We're all going there at 5 o'clock to see it, and we want you to join us."

"Me?"

41

"Sure, why not? It's always fun to look through houses for sale, don't you think?"

"I love doing that. Sometimes I go to open houses just to get ideas."

"That's how I came up with making that small, unused closet into a separate bar area."

"Mama, I want to see the house! Can I go too?"

"Of course. But no Sweet Pea this time."

We left a sad dog behind, and all climbed into my SUV to drive to what I now referred to as Cal's place. When we pulled onto the street, Mike commented, "It's so interesting to find these pockets of great housing all over the valley. This is a pretty cool area, Cal."

"Not bad, is it?" he responded.

As we drove further down the street, Isabella leaned forward. "Is this the house, Mama? This big house?"

"Yes, that's the one."

"It's so pretty... and big!"

The house was almost triple in size compared to my townhouse, so it was easy to see why Isabella would be entranced with it. "And, Mama, look at the garden in front!" she exclaimed as she hopped out of the car and ran forward.

We laughed at Isabella's enthusiasm. If she were the buyer, the real estate agent wouldn't have to make any effort to make the sale. The rest of us exited the car to meet Sylvia and introduce ourselves. Instead of beginning the tour inside the house, we walked to the back to show them what I thought was the most appealing aspect of the property. Looking at it for the second time only increased its beauty for me.

We walked by the pool, and Isabella said, "Don't worry, Grandfather, I already know how to swim," she stated in a tone that was supposed to set him at ease. We smiled at each other.

Virginia walked to the small house in the rear and asked, "Is this part of the property? How wonderful is this?"

Cal and I locked eyes.

"Yes, it is," said Sylvia. "Isn't it darling?"

"What will you do with it, Cal?" asked Virginia.

"I was thinking of renting it. Are you interested?" answered Cal.

Virginia's face crumpled, and her eyes watered. Her face reddened, and it was easy to see she was embarrassed. Cal looked mortified and held my eye as he realized his question had caught her off guard.

"I'm sorry. We can talk about it later," Cal whispered as he put his arm on her shoulder, comforting her.

Sylvia raised her voice, "Aw, right, everyone," she said, "Let's head back to the front of the house and begin the tour from the beginning, shall we?"

We all followed her, Virginia self-consciously close to Sylvia, leaving Cal to tag along with Mike, Isabella, and me.

Inside, we took our time going from room to room, gushing over each one. When we climbed upstairs, Isabella raced through all the rooms, taking a quick peek inside each one. Then, she ran to where we stood in the master room. "Grandfather, come with me. I want to show you my room."

We looked at each other in surprise. "Isabella, we aren't moving here; just Grandfather is. You do realize that, don't you?" I asked.

"I know, Mama. My room is for when I come here for a sleepover."

"Oh," I said, looking at Cal.

"Yes, show me which room is going to be yours." The idea seemed to please him, and he smiled and patted Isabella's head.

"C'mon, everyone. I want you to see it, too," Isabella said.

We all followed her to the bedroom toward the back overlooking the pool area. It was a darling room with a window seat and bookcases on either side. It looked feminine and perfect for a little girl. "You and Mike can sleep in the room next to me, and Virginia's room is over there," she said, pointing across the hall,

None of us said a word for a few seconds as we grasped what Isabella was doing. Again, she was trying to recreate her family around those of us she loved and felt safe having near her.

Cal was the first to move. "Well, then, I guess it's decided. Let's go downstairs and tell Sylvia she's just sold a house!"

"Yes, Grandfather, yes! Can I go tell her?"

"Sure," he said as she raced down the stairs and headed for the kitchen where Sylvia waited.

Putting his hand on Cal's shoulder, Mike asked, "Are you sure this is the house you want?"

"Yes, it's the perfect house for many reasons, Mike. The perfect family home, don't you think?" he asked, winking at me.

After Cal spoke with Sylvia, we piled into the car to return to my townhouse, which seemed mighty small after being in Cal's new home.

When we arrived home, Virginia announced she had to leave because she had other plans for the evening. Cal looked surprised but rallied. "Here, I'll walk you to your car."

When Cal came back into the house, his cheeks were pink. "Well?" I said. Did you two work things out?"

"I asked her to join me for dinner tomorrow night, but she reminded me we were already invited to Romano's house. So we're going the following night."

"I'm sorry if what you said upset her …."

He held his hand up and interrupted me. "No, none of that. We'll work out what's best for all of us. Don't worry," he said, patting me on the back.

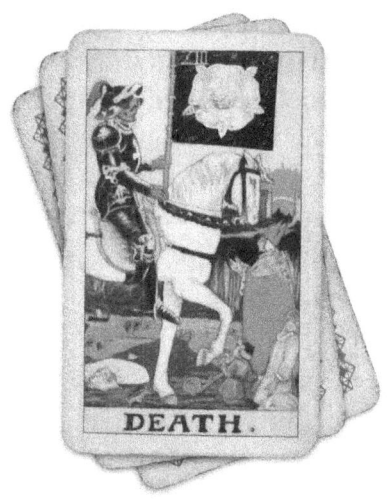

CHAPTER 10

I left Mike at home with Isabella while Cal and I headed to the construction site. We were the first ones there, and we walked over to where Red was leaning against his pickup truck. He looked familiar, but I couldn't place where I'd seen him before. "Good morning," I said. "Are you Red Scarvoni?"

"Yeah, so?" replied Red, eying me with disdain. "I know all about you, lady. What do you want?"

Cal took a step closer, protecting me. "We're meeting with your boss to review some of the materials used here. Care to join us?"

Romano and Mimi were coming onto the site, and we watched Red's face cloud with disgust when he saw Romano. "Nah, I haven't got time to deal with fairies."

A few steps behind Romano and Mimi was the owner of the construction company. Cal and I stepped forward to meet him, who quickly introduced himself as Anthony Carrera and held out his hand. Red turned away and began to fumble with his tools, pointedly ignoring his boss.

After the introductions, we all entered the restaurant's building. Cal began to poke around, trying to see what was beneath the plywood installed on the floor and walls. "Mimi, where are the slips for the restaurant?" he asked, holding out his hand.

Cal looked through them, and with each slip he pulled out, he went to a part of the building where the item should have been to see if it were a match. As Romano, Mimi, and I stood back, Anthony moved closer to Cal's side to watch every move he made. Their heads came together, nearly touching, as each pointed something out.

After a while, Cal approached us and said, "It all looks good here. Let's check the office building, shall we?"

The office building wasn't as far along in construction as the restaurant site. As before, the rest of us stood back and let Cal work with Anthony to distinguish between what was in place and what'd been billed. There were discrepancies galore during the days that Red had been in charge. At the beginning of the review, Anthony began to argue loudly, denying anything was amiss. But after Cal lost his temper and told Anthony to "get a grip on reality, man," things settled down.

"Where's Butch?" we asked as Cal and Anthony joined us.

"I pulled him off this job to head up another one."

"Anthony, we need him back here on this job," stated Cal in a tone that refused any argument.

Anthony lowered his head and nodded. "Okay."

Several of the crew had already pulled their vehicles onto the site and were starting to unload their tools. We said goodbye to Anthony and watched as he marched to where Red stood outside his truck, scowling at us. A wave of goosebumps crossed my body as I realized that, yet again, I was involved with another person who would soon be very unhappy about our taking a stand, unable to let things slide. I hoped he wouldn't be vengeful—like Jerry.

Cal and I said goodbye to Romano and Mimi, saying we'd see them later at Romano's house for dinner. Then we headed home. My spirits were low, and Cal sensed it. He patted my shoulder. "Are you okay?"

I nodded. "I don't trust Red. Why can't people be trusted to do the right thing?"

Cal chuckled.

"What? It's not funny!"

"My sweet girl, what's right? For one person, it's one thing; for another, it's something else."

I frowned at him, knowing what he said was true.

"I know what you mean, though," he conceded. "It's a tough world we live in today."

Appeased, I nodded.

We arrived back home in time to see Isabella off to school. She was excited because this was the day they could choose what to do to fulfill their community service obligation. It was going to be interesting to see what she'd pick.

Mike kissed me goodbye and called back to Cal, "Be careful, you two, and take plenty of water with you. The desert is sweltering this time of year."

Wanting to take advantage of the cooler morning air compared to the afternoon temperatures, Cal and I loaded into the car right after Mike left. We'd already put on sunscreen and had a large hat covering most of our faces. I also filled a knapsack with water, light enough to carry.

According to the map, we drove north on Route 15 and looked for the spot where we wanted to turn off. When I'd been on the school trip long ago, I remembered we had driven down a road from the highway toward one of the smaller mountains. It was somewhere along there that I recalled the stream and the pretty flowers.

Cal leaned forward in his seat. "There," he said and pointed to his right. The road we were looking for was just ahead, and we turned in. When we drove along it, dust flew everywhere and covered the car with its residue, making it hard to see. We continued, and when we reached the end of the road, we got out of the car and looked around. I knew right away that this wasn't the place I'd been to before. We decided to walk the area anyway. We came across what appeared to be the remains of a rabbit that a coyote probably had chewed on. I looked around to see where a coyote might hide during the hottest part of the day and couldn't come up with anything. The desert was a beast of its own making for many animals and its predators, simply with excessive heat during the day and the chill at night.

Instead of driving to another area of the desert, we decided to head home. We were hot and sticky, and I longed for a refreshing shower. After my shower, I made a list of what I wanted to buy at the grocery store, and Cal left me to drive to the realtor's office to complete some additional paperwork. I got home just in time to finish putting the groceries away before Isabella came through the door.

"Hi, Mama! Guess what I'm doing for community work."

"What, sweetheart?"

"I'm going to be helping out at the soup kitchen! And Tiffany is too."

"Well, that sounds good. You'll be able to help feed hungry people. Do you know which teacher will be there with you?"

"Not yet. Where's Grandfather? I want to tell him too." As if by magic, Cal stepped through the door. "Grandfather!" Isabella raced to his side and pulled him toward the kitchen. "Do you know what I am going to be doing?"

I let them go on their way while I went into my office. I loved writing my spiritual column for them, which always inspired me. I had to send out the latest *Women Living Well* magazine article. The newest take on the magazine was getting 'down and dirty' with what was happening in the world. I'd agreed to write about Las Vegas; however, that column had been put on hold for a while. They would test out the magazine's new slant with another column first.

When Isabella searched and found me, I said, "We've been invited to Romano's and Randy's house for dinner tonight. Randy's in a new walking cast and can move around on his own. Isn't that nice?"

Isabella nodded. "What are we going to wear?" she asked, hoping we'd have to go shopping for something new.

"What you have on is fine, or you can wear jeans."

Her face fell, and she pouted. Then we looked at each other and laughed because I'd caught her in her game of pretending to be upset.

When we arrived at Romano's, my eyes watered as I watched Randy awkwardly move to greet us, struggling to hide his pain. He'd saved my life when he pushed me away from a speeding car and took the full impact of the car himself. Because of that, I felt indebted to him.

Mike, reading my mind, put his finger across my lips. "Don't say a word, Rosie. It wasn't your fault," he whispered.

Sensitive to my feeling guilty for not having suffered what he had, Randy said, "Come here, Rosie, and give me a big hug." He enveloped me in a hug. Then he said, "Thank you for coming. I've missed you all."

Isabella cuddled up next to him and let him hug her. "I'm glad that you can walk again, Uncle Randy."

"Me too," smiled Randy. He put his hand on her shoulder and leaned on her as he led us into the living room, swinging his cast clumsily with each step.

Later, Romano poured all but Isabella a glass of champagne at the table. "Here's to Randy. So glad you're on the mend, my darling." We toasted each other and repeated the toast when he added, "And here's to my dearest friends."

We got a bit misty-eyed as we watched Romano fight back his tears. Then Isabella asked, "Is everyone going with us to Santa Fe for Thanksgiving, Mama?"

I was surprised she'd asked because I hadn't considered Thanksgiving plans yet. Usually, I would've made plans by now, but I had so many things on my mind that I had done nothing.

"Randy and I won't be able to make it. But we'll be there in spirit," said Romano.

"I'm sorry, but I'm going home to be with my father. He's not that well," added Mimi.

Isabella wore an expression of disbelief. She looked at Cal. "Grandfather, you'll be there, won't you?"

"I'm so sorry, Isabella, but I have plans."

Isabella's face fell. "What about Christmas?" she asked hopefully.

I put my hand on her shoulder. "We'll talk about it later, Isabella."

While eating, I thought about the holidays. Usually, I'd fly to Boston with Sweet Pea and stay with Karen. I wondered if she'd spend Thanksgiving with her new boyfriend this year. Karen, Nancy, Susannah, and I were sister-friends (more like sisters than friends) and had been college roommates at Cornell. We were close and used to try to spend the holidays together. But times had changed. I'd have to check with Karen because I didn't want her to spend the holiday alone. I'd heard already from both Nancy and Susannah. Nancy and her boyfriend would be in Idaho for both Thanksgiving and Christmas. Susannah and her husband had plans for Thanksgiving and were going away for Christmas.

It wasn't like me not to be highly organized for both holidays already. This year, everything was going to be different. It would be the first time Isabella, Mike, and I would be like a little family. We'd spend time with our new family in Santa Fe—Maria, the other half to raise Isabella, her husband Miguel, daughters Angela and Rosa, and the three little boys. Instead of the holidays being quiet with just Sweet Pea and me, these holidays would be over the top. I couldn't wait!

CHAPTER 11

S everal weeks flew by. Mike was settling into his new office space and involved in trying to locate the missing girl Cal had hired him to find. He was involved in another job as well. A large company in California had hired Mike to investigate the theft of some of their parts and supplies that had gone missing. He'd been away for almost a week and had identified the culprits—an inner ring of employees. Mike was due back the following day.

Cal had left for home a few days after signing for the house. Together, we'd gone out to the desert twice more to see if we could locate the area where Jerry implied more bodies rested. We had no luck.

I went to the construction site every day to check on the progress of my building and to compare the slips to any materials dropped off. Romano, Mimi, and I had gotten quite good at identifying the materials specified in the contract with those dropped off at the site. If we weren't sure, we asked Butch or one of the other workers for clarification. Although Butch treated me with barely concealed contempt, with him back as site manager, things seemed okay. However, I couldn't help but think that no matter where Red Scarvoni was working, he was cheating someone.

Isabella had brought Tiffany home with her a few times, and I had to give her credit, for she was far more patient with Tiffany than I was. Even Mike was more tolerant than me. It was difficult for me not to snap at her behavior.

I heard the school bus pull in and then Isabella's footsteps as she rushed through the door, waving a note from school. "Want to, Mama? Want to help too?"

"Here, let me see," I said, reaching for the note. It said that tomorrow, the foursome who'd chosen to work at the soup kitchen would begin at 9:00 a.m., and the school was looking for volunteer mothers. The note signed off with *Apologies for the short notice*. I hugged Isabella. "Sure, I'll volunteer. It should be fun."

Isabella smiled. "What should we make, Mama?"

"I think they'll have that lined up for us. I guess we'll have to wait and see if we can choose the menu down the road. I'll call to volunteer."

"I'll call Tiffany and tell her we'll pick her up. I don't think it'd be a good idea for her to arrive in a limo," she said knowingly.

"I'll be happy to pick her up. Just tell her I like to be there early, so be ready at 8:30 a.m. sharp."

The following morning, I got up and put on my jeans, ready for the soup kitchen. I went into my office to pay bills before Isabella joined me for breakfast. Not long after

I began, she skipped down the stairs with Sweet Pea at her heels, excited to begin her volunteer work. We ate cereal with fresh strawberries and hopped in the car to pick up Tiffany. I wanted to arrive at Tiffany's house a bit early as I expected she'd have nobody who'd check on her to make sure she was ready in time. I let Isabella knock on the door while I waited in the car. Soon the front door opened, and Isabella was ushered inside. I sat in the car disgruntled as I waited and waited. What was the matter with that family? They seemed to have no regard for others, I fumed.

I huffed and puffed in the car until I caught myself in my reaction. What was the matter with me? Things would work out as they worked out. Why was I getting so upset? The girls were still children. I closed my eyes and tilted my head back to relax. Suddenly, the car's back door opened and jolted me out of my relaxation. I turned to the girls and smiled, determined to be pleasant.

Tiffany didn't look happy. "Why did you have to come so early?" she scolded.

Isabella rolled her eyes at the same time I snapped, "Early? We're going to be lucky to get there on time."

"Geez, you don't have to bite my head off," she replied.

I bit my tongue and didn't respond. As we neared the soup kitchen, I saw people hanging around outside. I parked the car alongside the building, locked my purse in the car, and went inside. We were late. A lady behind the counter waved us forward and pointed to the aprons hanging on a hook. "Put on one of those and grab a hairnet. You'll help me serve. You girls go in the back and help the others prep for lunch."

Isabella and Tiffany hesitated.

I put on an apron and said, "Do as you were asked." And they left.

We were there to make lunch for the following day, the only day all the regular staff would have off. A volunteer would be there to serve it up.

The woman hastily introduced herself as Mabel and rushed to the door to let the people inside. Word must have gotten out because the line seemed endless as we handed scrambled eggs, toast, and an apple to each one. I was so busy I didn't have a chance to do more than quickly glance at each person. When all but two dawdlers were left, I looked around, surprised to see all ages sitting there. Some were families, and others looked as if they had been homeless for years. I couldn't begin to imagine how difficult it would be not to have a house of my own and go through what these people were enduring.

"How does it make sense for anyone to be homeless in a country as wealthy as ours?" I asked myself.

Much to my surprise, my grandmother's spirit responded, "No, it doesn't."

"Your first time here?" asked an older woman as she handed me her empty coffee mug.

I smiled. "It shows then, huh?"

"Yep," she said and wandered off.

I tried not to stare at the guests as they came to the wooden stand next to where I stood so they could return their coffee mugs. Two men looked dangerous to me—men I felt I needed to watch around Isabella and Tiffany. They reminded me that some homeless people had mental issues and could be dangerous if they were off drugs. I sighed. Life wasn't always easy, no matter who you were.

I went to the back, where the girls were prepping for lunch. "What are you fixing for lunch tomorrow?" I asked.

Isabella looked at me with sparkling eyes. "Goulash and I got a turn browning the meat."

"That's wonderful!"

"I get to help cook the macaroni, too," she added, pleased.

I introduced myself to the two women hovering over the girls who were cooking, and then I went to the woman at the sink, washing the dirty pots and pans. "Do you want help?"

She turned and smiled. "That'd be nice. I'm Mary Jane, Stephanie's mother."

"Nice to meet you. I'm Rosie, Isabella's mother." Out of the corner of my eye, I saw Isabella smile as I reached for a towel to dry the dishes.

"Oh, no, you don't! It's still my turn. You're going to have to wait until I'm finished," yelled Tiffany.

Deborah's mother stood beside her, scowling. "You girls must take turns, and your time is up, Tiffany." She reached for the wooden spoon, and simultaneously, she used her hip to push her aside and make room for the shy girl waiting her turn. I was impressed with her moves and winked when she looked my way.

"Tiffany, why don't you help me dry some of these dishes?" I asked, trying to get her attention away from the stove.

"No," she said and headed to the eating area in the front. I followed her to where she sat at one empty table. I put my hand on her shoulder. I could tell she was upset.

"Mind if I join you?"

She grimaced and bobbed her head, and I sat down. "Tiffany, if you treat others how you want to be treated, your life will be so much easier. You know that, don't you?"

She looked at me and said nothing for a few minutes— just hung her head. "Can we go home now?" she asked.

"Afraid not, kiddo. We still have work to do. Let's go back in there together and help clean up the dishes, okay?"

"Aw, right," she said, flouncing back into the kitchen. "Here," she said, handing me a towel. "You take the wet towel; I want the dry one."

Isabella heard this as she came over to help us. We looked at each other and smiled. Tiffany was a handful; there was no way around it.

After we all finished preparing lunch for the next day and cleaning up, we went our separate ways. I dropped Tiffany off at her house, and Isabella and I went shopping at the mall. On the way there, I received a voicemail message from my sister-friend Karen asking if she could invite herself to Santa Fe for Thanksgiving. I immediately texted back, "Glad to have you with us!"

As we searched the sales for a dress for Isabella, I couldn't get Karen off my mind. Despite all her fun-loving ways, Karen's relationships had not been easy. While in college, she was somewhat naïve and allowed a boyfriend to overpower her with his demands and needs, which nearly caused her to have a breakdown when he began to stalk her. It wasn't until she confided in us about what was going on that we could trap him by taking videos of him in action. We reported him to the police since the school hadn't responded to her complaints. We also kept several threatening letters he had written her, which led the police to call in his parents to discuss his problem. The school finally got involved, and he didn't return the following semester, much to our relief. That whole thing killed dating for Karen for quite some time. The last time we sister-friends had been together, Karen had been excited to announce she was dating one of the other teachers in her school.

While Isabella tried on a few dresses, I stepped aside and called Karen, hoping I could speak to her in person instead of reaching her voicemail. She picked up on the third ring. "Hey, Girlfriend! What's going on?" I asked.

"Rosie, I need a few days to collect myself. Eric has asked me to marry him...."

"Wait! Did I hear you say Eric asked you to marry him?"

"Yes. That's why I need to get away...."

"Karen, am I missing something? Because he asked you to marry him is why you have to get away?"

"Exactly. I knew you'd understand."

"But...."

"I've taken a few days off. If that's okay with you, I'll make reservations to fly into Santa Fe the Monday before Thanksgiving. I'll fly home Saturday night to prepare for school the following Monday."

I heard someone calling her name. "Sorry, I have to run, but thanks so much for everything, Rosie. I can't wait to see you!"

"Wait! Send me your itinerary, and I'll pick you up at the airport, okay?"

I ended the call, somewhat confused. I'd have to wait to see what was going on. I decided to call Nancy and Susannah, our other sister-friends, and tell them what was happening. Nancy did not answer, so it ended up that it was just Susannah and me on the call. I told her about my conversation with Karen.

"What do you think is going on with her?" asked Susannah.

"I dunno. There must be something more than being nervous about getting married, right?

"Maybe she's going out there to ask you in person to be her Maid of Honor."

"Wouldn't she want all of us? No, I think it's something else. We'll have to wait and see."

We arrived home from the mall with a few small Thanksgiving decorations that'd be easy to pack and take to Santa Fe—napkins, candles, and napkin holders. Isabella picked out two pairs of shoes, and because she was growing so fast, we'd have to do some serious shopping soon to buy jeans, tops, and jackets to replace those becoming too small for her. I was excited about the upcoming holiday, although I now would have to work it out with Mike and Isabella to leave early for Santa Fe so that I could spend a few extra days with Karen. We sister-friends always had an open invitation to each other's homes, but Karen had to be struggling over something for her not to have considered the logistics now that Isabella and Mike were part of my life. We'd work it out, though.

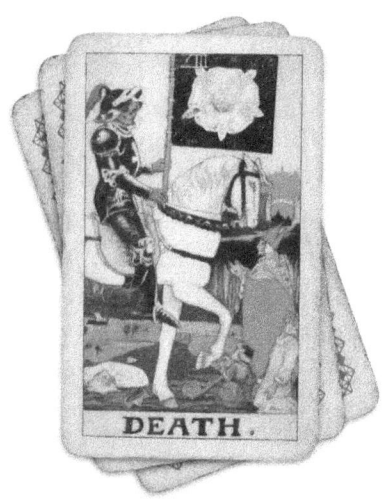

CHAPTER 12

When Sweet Pea began to bark, I knew Mike had arrived home from California. I raced downstairs to meet him. He pushed through the back door, and his face lit up when he saw me standing there. I rushed forward and snuggled into his waiting arms. "I'm so glad to see you! I've missed you."

"And I'm glad to see you!" he said, placing his hand on my lower back and pulling me tight against him. "Ah, my queen." His kiss was long and sweet, melting my body in all the right places.

"Hmm," I sighed. We listened as Isabella and Sweet Pea came noisily down the stairs. Sweet Pea raced in and jumped on Mike, vying for his attention. As Isabella neared, both Mike and I opened our arms to include her in a hug.

"Now that is what I call a greeting," laughed Mike, holding us close.

Isabella stepped back. "Mama and I had our first day at the soup kitchen, and guess what we cooked?"

I winked at Mike, and he smiled. "Let me get inside, and then you can tell me all about it," he said as he moved his suitcase to the bottom of the steps going upstairs.

"You two go ahead. I'll put the chicken in the oven and fix a salad for tonight. When you finish, Mike, why don't you pour us a nice glass of wine before dinner?"

My heart was happy. Things were quiet, with no more murders, just the missing girl Mike was trying to track down. I intended to go out to the desert tomorrow to give it another try to locate the area I remembered from the past— the one Jerry indicated might have other bones there.

While Mike and I sat with our wine, I told him about Karen arriving in Santa Fe early for Thanksgiving.

"Does that mean you'll want us all there early, too?" he asked.

"Well, Isabella has school the Monday and Tuesday before Thanksgiving, so I thought …."

"Ah, you want me to stay with Isabella while you fly out to meet Karen?"

"Well, I …"

"No worries. I've got it covered."

"Oh, Mike, thanks so much. I'll make reservations for Sunday night. That way, I can prepare the house for you and meet with Maria to review our plans. Let's talk this over with Isabella at dinner, okay?"

At first, Isabella was silent. Then she became excited, "You mean I'll get to meet one of your sister-friends?"

I nodded, pleased with her excitement.

"And Mike will be here with me until it's time for us to go to Santa Fe?"

"Yes, sweetheart."

"Cool," she said with a smile.

I looked at Mike, and he winked at me.

After letting Sweet Pea outside for her nightly bathroom duty, I went upstairs to tuck Isabella into bed. I stretched beside her and asked, "Is everything okay with you, kiddo?"

"Yes, Mama. Can Nica and Angela spend the night with me? Can we have a sleepover?"

"I don't see why not. Why don't we plan for the day after Thanksgiving? I heard you talking to Angela earlier, and Maria told me they would invite you to spend Wednesday night with them. Are you okay with that?"

She turned to me with sparkling eyes. "I guess one night there won't kill me, right, Mama?"

I laughed. "I certainly hope not."

Isabella giggled. "You're so funny, Mama."

"Maria also told me that they were adding on a master bedroom suite, and you and Angela will be taking over their old room. That's nice, isn't it?"

"Yes, and Angela and I get to pick out the color paint we want. She wants pink."

"What color do you want?"

"I wanted a pale yellow, but I don't care. I won't spend that much time there so Angela can have what she wants."

"That works, then, right?"

"Yup," she smiled.

"Goodnight, Little One." I used her name of a lifetime ago when I had been her older sister, Little Bird, and we'd been part of a Navajo tribe living in Santa Fe. "I love you to the moon and beyond!"

Isabella smiled. "Goodnight, Mama. I love you too." I bent over to kiss her, then Sweet Pea, goodnight, and left.

J.S. Peck

My heart filled with joy when I entered my bedroom and saw Mike in bed, waiting for me. Our lovemaking had reached a point where we knew how to pleasure each other, and to say that Mike had become a master lover was an understatement. I was thrilled he enjoyed my entire body and showed me how much in so many ways. That night I knew it would be no exception.

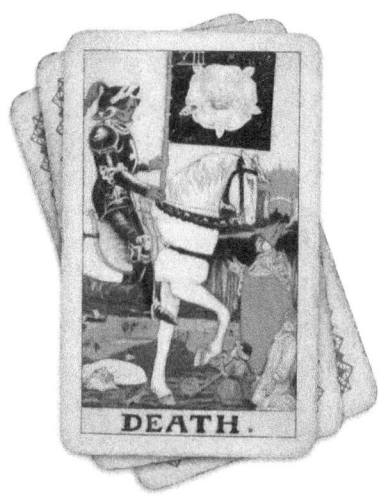

CHAPTER 13

T he following day, after we kissed Isabella good-bye, Mike and I loaded into the car to drive out into the desert. The night before, I'd had a vivid dream about the field trip I'd taken in high school. Something in it stirred a memory about the break in the background mountain that made me believe I could now locate the area we were searching out.

"No, keep driving, Mike. A little bit further."

"Are you sure?"

"Yup, keep going. There!" I pointed out. "Go slow. Let's see if there is a way in."

A car behind us beeped, and Mike opened his window and waved him ahead.

"Right here, Mike! Pull in here."

"Wow, I would've missed it. This road's very old. Are you sure this is the right one?"

"I'm pretty sure it is. Look further in. It looks like the road is still being used."

"Alright then, let's give it a try."

As we drove down the road, I sat on the edge of my seat and closed my eyes to recall my dream and the break in the mountain. As we continued, I opened my eyes and trained them on the spot. Without warning, we came to a place that ended any regular road going any further. We got out of the car and looked around. I wandered to a clump of stray wildflowers, barely alive, and called for Mike. "Come here. Doesn't this look like a dried-up creek to you?"

He stood beside me. "It sure does. Let's see if we can follow it. Why don't you go one way, and I'll go the other?"

I turned left and followed what would've been upstream, and Mike went the opposite way. Old feelings came back. High school had not been a great time for me. I'd been bullied for my grandmother's and my psychic abilities and for being different… not happy memories. Perhaps that was why that school trip had been a significant time for me. Amid all the unpleasantness of daily school life, I'd seen the beauty of the desert through the beautiful wildflowers that'd bloomed there in late spring.

I walked along, lost in thought, until I came to a site where it was easy to see someone had been digging. There were two empty holes, with dirt piled beside each of them. But it looked as if there could be more to discover. But what caused goosebumps to cover my body was seeing a visible freshly dug site, still slightly rounded in the middle. Foreboding washed over me as I realized I'd found the spot Jerry must have meant.

"Mike, over here! Bring the shovel," I hollered.

"You found it?" he asked in disbelief when he came into view.

"Look at these empty holes. And this one; it's something new, don't you think?"

"Yeah, it looks like it. Let's see what we have here." Mike went first to the open holes and searched for anything that might give us a clue to what'd been buried. "These both appear pretty clean, but we'll have Forensics take a look. They'll have to search the whole area."

"Aren't we going to see what's inside this new one?"

Knowing I was curious to see what, if anything, had been buried there, Mike moved to my side. "We might as well look …."

I became mesmerized by the movement of each shovelful Mike took. The dry dirt was easy for him to move, and before long, we saw first a hand, then an arm, and then the head of a decaying body. The body had not been dead that long since some of the bones still held some pieces of flesh and clothing. A thought instantly flashed across my mind. "Who's the girl you're looking for, Mike?"

He studied me. "What made you think of her?"

"I don't know. Just a thought."

"Well, we'll find out soon enough. I'll give the police chief a call right now. I hope you weren't planning on doing much today because we'll be busy here for a while."

"If Jerry knew there were more bones here, do you think he also knows about the latest corpse? And if he does, do you think he knows the killer?"

"That's something we can hopefully find out."

When we got home, Mike and I were both tired and dirty. Besides the fresh grave, it'd been disheartening to discover three others filled with bones. They looked similar in age to the two sets of bones dumped at the construction site, so I was guessing they'd been killed around the same time. Testing would determine that.

Virginia met us at the door, and Mike left us to shower. Virginia had become more like a loveable aunt than a housekeeper or babysitter. I thought she was becoming much more than that to Cal, and I was curious to see if they were communicating. "Anything new from Cal?"

She smiled as she poured me a glass of iced mint tea. "Cal called yesterday to say that he was sick of deciding what to pack up and what to sell. He said he would call you to see if you and I will drive down to help him decide about a few of his mother's things."

"Really? That's fine with me after we get back from Thanksgiving. So I see you two are growing your relationship, then? That's great. You're going to move into the little house, right?"

"Yes, it'll be perfect for me. Thanks for all you did to put that in place. Cal told me about it."

"Well, it makes perfect sense to me. Good for both of you, don't you think?"

"I do," she smiled.

"You know, I'm going to love having both of you just around the corner from us."

"Yes, that'll be nice," she agreed. "How can I help you before you leave for Santa Fe?"

"Well, Mike is going to be working with the police chief to identify the new bones that we found. Roberto has asked Mike to give him a hand, which he's more than willing to do. If you remember, we put together a lot of paperwork on girls found missing around four or five years ago when we went looking for what happened to Susan. Being at the police station also provides Mike more support to track down the girl he's looking for who went missing several weeks ago."

"It's so sad to learn of more bodies."

"Yes, isn't it? It seems that there are so many people who get lost in the shuffle of life, whether it's murder or addiction or mental illness, or human trafficking. All of it is sad to me."

"How about if we get a start on baking for the holidays?" asked Virginia. "I'm happy to share a few special family cookie recipes if you'd like."

"How nice! I'm sorry you won't be joining us for Thanksgiving. But maybe you'll think about spending Christmas with us?"

"That sounds lovely. I'll have to see how things work out."

I knew she meant how things worked out with Cal, but I let it go. I decided to take a shower and hopefully wash off the desert dirt and disappointment of finding more bones and a fresh grave.

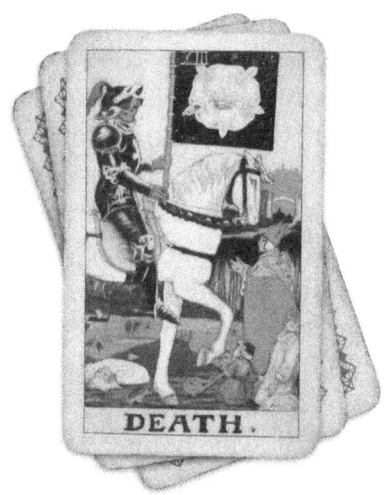

CHAPTER 14

A t the airport, I nervously said goodbye to Mike and Isabella. I was torn about leaving the two most important people in my life, and I wasn't used to the unease it brought about. I felt a swirl of air around me. *"This is what love is all about. Just trust and let things be,"* my grandmother whispered beside me. I knew she was right, so I waved one last time and went inside to wait for takeoff.

My flight was easy. If we were traveling back and forth between Las Vegas and Santa Fe a lot, we'd have to do something about transportation. Perhaps store a car in Albuquerque. After landing in Albuquerque, I quickly went to the car rental agency and picked up my car.

When I pulled into the driveway of my Santa Fe home, a feeling of satisfaction washed over me as I considered my situation compared to a year ago. How lucky I was to have such beautiful people now in my life in addition to my dear sister-friends. There were no words to describe how I felt about my new relationships with Mike, Isabella, Maria, her family, Grandmother, Cal, Virginia, Romano, Randy, Mimi, and Brian. My heart filled with love for all of them. And yet, as I let myself into the house, a flash of worry crossed my mind. I had loved before and had lost those dearest to me in unexpected ways—my parents, grandmother, and fiancé—and I didn't want anything to happen to any of the people I loved. But, then again, who did?

I was pleased to look around and see the house all in order. We'd left it that way before we'd returned to Las Vegas. In the morning, I'd go to the store and buy most of the food we needed for the week. I'd already ordered a fresh turkey online and would pick it up on Wednesday. I was also going to meet with the sheriff in the morning before I picked up Karen at the airport. Coyote had statement papers for me to sign regarding what'd happened when his nephew had tried to kidnap Isabella last summer. His nephew had been hooked on drugs, and to pay for them, he'd been dealing with unsavory types whom Coyote, Mike, and I thought were connected to child sex trafficking. As far as I knew, his nephew was still in rehab, and Coyote hadn't been able to get him to share what he knew so that we could destroy the ring of people involved.

Before I did anything else, I wanted to call Mike and Isabella to tell them I was missing them already. After talking, I unpacked, put away my suitcase, and crawled into bed. It was so quiet compared to Las Vegas that I wasn't sure I'd be able to sleep, but when I woke up eight hours later, I'd been proved wrong.

It was colder in Santa Fe, and I was glad I'd brought my down jacket. After grocery shopping at Albertson's, I went home to put the things away before meeting with Coyote. I didn't have too much time left before I'd have to leave to pick up Karen at the airport.

"Good morning!" I said to the policeman at the front desk, who flashed me a smile. I continued toward the back to Coyote's office.

"Hi, Coyote! I'm here to sign those papers you wanted me to sign. My friend, Karen, is coming into town for a few days, so I'm picking her up at the airport." As an afterthought, I added, "I think you'll like her."

He looked at me oddly, then politely said, "I'm sure I will."

As I hopped into my car and headed to the airport in Albuquerque, I wondered why I'd even mentioned Karen to Coyote. I still hadn't figured out why she was coming to Santa Fe to talk to me. What had happened to have her make this trip? Knowing Karen, it had to be something interesting.

I had only minutes to spare when I pulled into the airport parking garage. I ran my way into the baggage claim area. I hunted for the marque where the incoming flights were listed and the coordinated carousels for luggage pickup, where we'd agreed to meet. I needed to be at the right one to find her among all the incoming passengers.

As I stood there, I felt goosebumps all over my body. I turned, and my heart froze. Coming down the escalator into the baggage area was Johnny, my former boss from the Purple Passion Lounge in Las Vegas. He didn't see me, and I didn't want him to. I immediately turned into the bathroom alcove, connected to the baggage area, and stood out of view. Johnny moved along with the other passengers and carried a large executive overnight bag over his shoulder. He continued by the baggage carousels, obviously not needing to collect any additional baggage. He smiled wide as he was greeted by a fairly tall man dressed in a black overcoat. When they shook hands, I thought I saw the same scorpion tattoo on the tall man's hand that had been on two of the Mexican men who'd been murdered in Santa Fe. When I looked again, I couldn't make it out and wondered if I had conjured it up.

After Johnny passed and it was safe for me to move, I looked out again into the crowd. There was Karen. When she saw me, she made her way forward without any joyous little dance or arms waving above her head as usual.

"How was your flight?" I asked.

"Like them all. Long and boring."

I held up her left hand. "Where's your engagement ring?"

Karen looked embarrassed. "Well, that's just it. I'm not sure I want to be engaged, much less married... at least to him."

"What are you saying? I thought he was the love of your life!"

We grabbed her suitcase from the carousel and walked to the parking garage to get the car. After we buckled up, I asked, "Do you want to talk about it?"

"Not right now, if you don't mind. I need a little time to sort things out."

"Of course. No problem."

As we drove into Santa Fe, Karen came alive. As I watched her take in everything around her, it was nearly impossible to remember how down in the dumps she'd been earlier. "Wow! What a place! Look at those mountains over there! Beautiful, just beautiful," she sighed.

"You haven't seen anything yet. Wait until we get closer to town!"

"Oh, my God! It's so strange. Everything looks familiar to me, Rosie. I'd swear I've been here before if I didn't know better." She turned to look at me. "I love it!"

I didn't say it aloud, but I wondered whether she had lived here in a past life too. We pulled into the center of town, and I suggested, "Let's park, and I'll show you around a bit. We'll grab lunch at the little Mexican café that's so good. Is that okay with you?"

"Sure. That sounds great."

I pulled into a parking spot along the street that edged the Historic Plaza. I watched Karen's eyes light up as she looked all around. "How adorable! She turned to me with the first genuine smile since arriving in New Mexico.

We walked around for just a short time because we were both hungry. We ate at my favorite new restaurant, and Karen commented on how good the food was. Afterward, I said, "If you don't mind, let's walk over to the sheriff's office so I can tell him about seeing Johnny. It's just down the street."

When we got to his office, I greeted the deputy, who tipped his head to go on back, indicating Coyote was there. Karen said, "You go ahead. I'll wait here."

I surprised Coyote, who had not been expecting me. "Hi there, Coyote! When I picked up Karen at the airport, I saw one of my former bosses coming down the escalator. Johnny is one of the ones who was involved in child sex trafficking at the Purple Passion Lounge. I can't think his being here is anything good. I thought you should know."

"Well, that's certainly not good news. What's his name?"

"Johnny Cardoza."

"Thanks for the warning. I'll let my sheriff friend in Albuquerque know too."

"Come meet my friend, Karen," I urged. "She's waiting for me out front."

Karen was reading a brochure about Santa Fe she'd picked up at one of the stores we'd visited. She was completely unaware of us standing in the doorway. I felt a flash of energy behind me and stepped aside to let Coyote through. A light flush crept across his face as I looked at him, staring at Karen.

I called out, "Hey, Karen! I'd like you to meet our sheriff, Coyote."

Coyote took several steps forward to shake Karen's hand in greeting. She was so engrossed in reading the brochure clutched in her hand that she must not have heard us. She glanced up, seemingly reluctant to be disturbed, and Coyote's face flushed even deeper at her unintentional rudeness. When she realized her faux pas, she stood up and reached for his hand at the same time he was pulling it back, making her off balance. She almost fell on top of him. He reached out to catch her, making their awkward, clumsy embrace fascinating to see. I was surprised at Coyote's reaction, for it was apparent he was smitten with her, while Karen showed little response to him in return. It'd be interesting to see how that played out because Coyote was anything but a frivolous person.

Coyote stiffly said, "Nice to meet you, Karen," before turning away. As he walked past me, he mouthed, "What?" at my questioning glance.

I shook my head. "Nothing."

When we got outside, Karen was oblivious to my questioning expression of what she'd thought about Coyote. I never said a word about what I'd witnessed, for she seemed unaware that anything unusual had occurred. That was not like her.

"Let's take your things to the house so you can unpack and settle in," I suggested.

Once there, I showed Karen the guest room where she'd be staying. "Take your time to settle in, and I'll meet you in the kitchen when you're through."

Since we had eaten a late lunch, I took out fresh fruit, a soft brie cheese, and rice crackers and then cracked open a chilled bottle of Sauvignon Blanc.

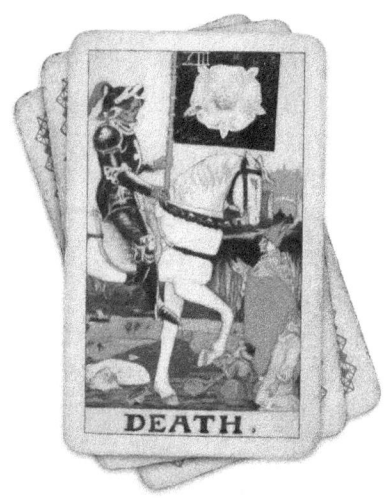

CHAPTER 15

❙❙ Shall we sit and enjoy ourselves with a glass of wine?" I asked when Karen joined me.

"That sounds heavenly," she responded, plopping down in one of the two chairs before the fireplace.

"Girlfriend, is everything okay with you?" I asked, impatient to hear what was going on in her world. We sat silently for a few minutes, each relaxed and enjoying our time together.

"I don't know if what I say to you will make any sense," she said. Taking a deep breath in, she continued. "You know me so well, Rosie, from when we first met as roommates in college until now. I've changed a lot, mainly because of your help and that of our other sister friends. And some therapy, too, of course. I no longer am the all-consuming people pleaser. I've learned to know who I am and love myself, imperfections and all."

When she looked at me, I asked, "So what's the problem?"

"Here, I have a chance to be married to a very nice man, and I don't think I can do it."

"Do you love him?" I asked.

"Yes, I do love him." She paused. "Just not in the way that makes for a long, happy marriage…."

"What do you mean?"

"It'd be a very safe and secure relationship because we'd both be teaching school, going to church on Sunday, and afterward, visiting his parents, who are very nice but boring people. We'd be doing all the routine things that have already become established and now seem set in stone."

I nodded my head to acknowledge what she'd said, but I remained silent.

"Is it wrong to want more?" she demanded. She was quiet for a minute before adding, "And another thing, although I know Eric loves me, he isn't very passionate," she burst out with her cheeks glowing red.

"Ahh…"

"I do not want a "bad boy" like all the young girls want, but I want to be with someone who isn't so predictable…."

"Have you discussed your feelings with him?"

"Yes. I've tried to change things and not have everything planned and scheduled, but it doesn't work for Eric. When I tried to explain what I need in a relationship, he told me, 'What you see is what you get.' Then he said he wants an answer to his marriage proposal by Christmas." Tears rolled down her face.

"Was he upset with you?"

"I think he was more hurt than upset. I hated doing that to him. I know how it is to have someone feel disappointed in who you are…."

"May I ask you a personal question?"

"Sure, Rosie, ask away," she sniffled.

"So because you want more in this relationship than what appears it can become, do you feel obligated to marry Eric simply because that's what he wants?"

"Ouch!" After being quiet for a few minutes, she said, "But you are so right. That's how I used to act with any male attention, isn't it?"

"Something to think about…." I said as I got up to get a Kleenex for her. I returned with the box of tissues and handed it to her.

She sniffled some more. We sat back in our chairs and were quiet until she asked, "Do Susannah and Nancy know I'm here?"

"Yes, they do. They're concerned about you and send their love. I said we'd try to get hold of them tomorrow so they'd know you're okay."

The following day, I woke to my phone ringing. It was early, and it was Mike calling. He sounded frantic. "Good morning, baby. Do I need to pack for Isabella, or can she do it herself? And what about Sweet Pea? Does she need medicine to fly, or will she be okay in the carrier without it?"

"Whoa! Slow down," I said as I tried to hold back a chuckle. "I've never heard you so rattled before ..."

He began to laugh. "It's just that I'm not used to traveling with a little girl and a dog. You're the one who takes care of everything when we're together. I want to make sure we're all set to fly out of here later."

"You'll be fine. Isabella knows what to pack. We went over everything before I left. She knows what to do with Sweet Pea as well, so other than you packing for yourself, everything should be all set. And your rental car is all ordered and should be waiting for you at the airport."

"That's just what I needed to hear. How's Karen doing, by the way?"

"Well, she's got a big decision—to marry Eric or not."

"That's not an easy decision for her?"

"Nope, it's not. Any news on the latest body?"

"Still waiting on the DNA tests."

"It's going to be interesting to find out who it is."

"I can't believe it is the one I'm looking for, but stranger things have happened."

"Well, handsome, I see it's time for Isabella to wake up for school. I'd better let you go."

"I'm looking forward to seeing you tonight. Love you, Rosie."

"Love you, too, Mike."

I wandered to the kitchen and was surprised to see Karen sitting at the counter. She smiled. "Where do you keep the coffee?"

"In the freezer. That's supposed to keep it fresher. Here, I'll get it."

"A nice fresh cup of coffee sounds wonderful."

"What would you like to do today?"

"How about shopping in some of those cute little stores we saw yesterday?"

"Sounds good to me. I want to introduce you to Grandmother if she's at the Palace of the Governors."

"Okay. I'm game."

CHAPTER 16

I parked the car alongside the street across from the Palace of Governors. Although I wasn't surprised, I was pleased to see Grandmother sitting with the other Native American Indians selling their wares. With all her psychic abilities, she probably knew we'd be coming to see her. As we crossed the street and came closer, her face lit up. She gave us a wide toothless grin and scrutinized Karen. I hurried to her, bending low and kissing her on each cheek.

"Hello, Grandmother—my mother."

"My daughter," she replied, kissing my hand. "Come forward, child," she said, holding her other hand out to Karen.

Bending down and speaking Tewa, Karen said, "Good morning, Grandmother. May the sun shine its light upon you with many blessings."

Grandmother's face creased with delight. She responded in Tewa, "The sun's blessings are many today."

As I watched them, it was apparent there was a connection between the two. Karen's face was glowing. She looked stunning with rosy cheeks, dark eyes, and dark hair flowing around her. For the first time since arriving in Santa Fe, she looked happy. I'd forgotten that one of Karen's studies and term papers written for college was about the Navajo Indian tribes of the West and their Tewa language. They'd already switched to English when I heard Karen say, "Yes, Grandmother, coming here is like being home again."

Grandmother flashed me a look, not needing to say anything because I understood her thoughts. We said goodbye and then stopped at a small café for Mexican coffee—little more than coffee with cinnamon—and a freshly baked churro—a Mexican donut.

"Do you know what you will do yet, Karen?"

"Simply being here is changing my whole way of thinking. There is wide open space here, whereas Boston is filled with buildings surrounded by winding old cow paths lined with trees. That makes it nearly impossible to see more than the sky right above. Of course, there is the ocean, a glory all by itself. But I must tell you, I'm falling in love with Santa Fe …."

"You're not simply thinking of running away, are you?"

Karen punched me on the shoulder in a friendly way. "I know it probably looks that way, but I mean it. I love this place."

When we had exhausted ourselves poking through many of the shops, I suggested, "Let's pop in and see Coyote. He wasn't too happy that my former boss is here in New Mexico. I want to see if he's heard anything more."

"Okay."

Coyote's smile widened when he saw Karen behind me as we entered his office. "Hey there!"

Coyote said something in Tewa, and Karen blushed. I looked at him and asked, "What did you say?"

Karen blushed. "You are as beautiful as the rising sun."

"Very poetic. I'm impressed," I said, looking at Coyote.

He was not acting at all like the rugged cowboy his appearance gave. What was it about a man that made him act so foolish when a beautiful woman was around? I knew it was not because of me as I watched a silent exchange between Coyote and Karen. I cleared my throat and said, "I just wanted to see if you'd heard anything about my former boss?"

"Nothing yet," he answered, his eyes still on Karen.

"I also wanted to tell you that Mike and Isabella will arrive tonight." With no response from Coyote, I added, "Well then... I guess we'd better be on our way and let you get back to what you were doing,"

"Has Karen met Grandmother yet?" Coyote asked me.

"Yes, I have, and she's wonderful," Karen answered.

Coyote looked deep into her eyes and smiled. "Good." What was going on? How did this happen? I couldn't miss that there, indeed, was something going on between the two of them. As we walked down the hallway toward the front, Coyote asked, "Would you ladies and Mike like to be my guest for dinner tomorrow night?"

Karen and I looked at each other. I nodded while Karen said, "That would be lovely, Coyote."

"Rosie, how about the same restaurant in the Eldorado Hotel where you and Isabella ate? I'll make reservations for 7 o'clock, okay? Do you mind meeting me there? I'll be coming from a meeting with the mayor." Again, we nodded in agreement. "Okay then," he said, obviously delighted.

Once outside, I said, "I don't know what hold you have over him, Karen, but he's certainly intrigued with you. I think it's time to get the cards out. What do you say?"

"First, though, let's go back to the last shop we were in so I can look at that dress I was considering, okay?"

I chuckled and followed her into the store, thinking there was nothing like a new, sexy dress to make you feel even more beautiful.

When we returned to the house, I pulled out some sliced ham and cheese to make a sandwich for a late lunch. It would be something to tide us over until dinner time. As we were eating, Karen said, "Okay, Rosie. Time to get out the cards! Remember the last time you read them for me? You said there were one, maybe two lovers coming to me?"

"Yes. We already know about the first love. And I think we already know something about the second one, don't we?"

Karen smiled shyly. "I think we might."

I got my tarot cards out. While holding them between the palms of my hands, I closed my eyes, energizing them. I stayed in that position for several minutes and then took them to the kitchen table where Karen was already seated. I shuffled and re-shuffled them several times. I finally laid them down on the table, face down.

"Karen," I ordered, "Cut the cards twice coming toward you."

I picked up the middle pile, then the first and last. As I laid the cards out, I said a prayer, asking for guidance from the highest energy of all, the love energy.

I turned each card up one by one and discussed what I saw. The Two of Cups card, meaning shared joy; the

King of Cups card, representing the fulfillment of joy; and several other positive cards. At first, I was startled to see the Death card, but when I had no foreboding chills, I realized it didn't mean murder this time. It showed the death of Karen's current relationship with her boyfriend. Since the Death card also said a new beginning, I knew without question that this card signified her new relationship with Coyote.

We talked about life and how it brings us new adventures every day. Sometimes a simple thought or without conscious thought results in experiences we never imagined. I smiled to myself and thought that was certainly true. I was amazed, for I would never have guessed Karen's being here would provide her a great love in her life. Coyote, no less! I only hoped she'd follow her heart and not do anything she'd regret later. I knew she was still struggling with feelings, but only time would tell what she'd decide to do.

My heart felt complete when Mike, Isabella, and Sweet Pea walked through the door later that night. Sweet Pea raced to Karen, jumped in her lap, and placed her paws on her shoulders, giving her kisses. Karen laughed as Isabella stood by my side and watched. When Karen looked our way, she said, "And who is this beautiful little princess?"

Isabella smiled but said nothing.

"Isabella, meet Karen, one of my sister-friends."

"Hi, Karen. I have sister-friends too."

"You're lucky then because sister-friends are the best kind of friends."

"I know," she answered with a smile.

Mike pulled me against his side, wrapping his arm around me. "Hi, Karen. How goes it?"

"Not too bad," she smiled.

"Really? That's good," he said, somewhat surprised. Mike sat with Karen while I went with Isabella to help her unpack her suitcase before she got ready for bed. Then I joined Mike and Karen in the living room, where they'd been quietly talking.

"Would you like me to fix a nightcap?" I asked them.

"Not for me," said Karen. "I'm going to get ready for bed myself. It's been a long day."

"A nightcap sounds nice," answered Mike, following me into the kitchen.

"How was your flight?"

"Interesting. A small girl and a dog seem to bring about a lot of attention."

I knew what he meant. "Hopefully, Sweet Pea did okay?"

"Yeah, everything was fine."

"Any news on the latest body?"

"Still waiting on the DNA. Hey, you! Come here and give me a proper welcome home kiss," he commanded.

I laughed. "I want more than that."

"No problem," he said as he pressed me against him, letting me know the certainty of what was to come.

When we finished sipping our drinks, I looked in on Isabella to say goodnight, and Karen was reading to her from an iPad she held. I looked at the two of them and thought how alike they were. Beautiful and lively, ready to face the world with joy even after all that'd happened in their lives. I reflected on one particular time when that was not the case for Karen. I was glad she was in a different place today despite the upset she was going through with her boyfriend back east.

I walked to where they were lying in bed and kissed the top of each head. "Goodnight, you beauties of the West. You queens of Santa Fe."

That saying was an adaption from the Cider Hill Rules, where Dr. Wilbur Larch said, "Goodnight, you princes of Maine. You kings of New England." Karen immediately recognized it and smiled.

"Not too late, you two. We have a busy day tomorrow," I urged.

"Okay, Mama."

"Sweet dreams then."

My stomach churned with excitement, knowing Mike was waiting for me in the bedroom. He made me feel like the most beautiful and loved woman in the world. Who could ask for more than that?

CHAPTER 17

T he next morning, we woke up, and no one stopped all day long, getting ready for Thanksgiving the next day. We extended the dining room table, which would be able to hold all of us, thank goodness. Isabella set the table with place cards; Mike ran to the store to buy booster seats for the little boys and then went to pick up the fresh turkey I'd ordered and some beer and wine.

Much to our delight, Maria and Angela decided to join us. So it was the five of us—Maria, Angela, Isabella, Karen, and me. We made the stuffing, a white potato casserole, a sweet potato casserole, a new broccoli casserole, a pumpkin pie, and an apple pie for the next day. Maria would bring Chili Relleno for all of us and tacos for the kids. We'd serve vanilla ice cream with the pastry. We laughed and had such a wonderful girlfriend time that we were sorry to have it end. Then after we cleaned up, Isabella left with Maria and Angela for the promised sleepover at their house. Friday night, all three girls—Isabella, Nica, and Angela— would have a sleepover with us.

"Thank God we don't have to cook tonight," I told Karen and Mike. "It's nice of Coyote to invite us to dinner, isn't it, Karen?" I teased so that I could watch her face flush pink. We chuckled, happy with the thought.

"Well, girls, you'd better get ready. I know how long it takes," said Mike.

"Oh, you do, do you?" I asked as I wrapped my arms around him.

He kissed me on the tip of my nose and patted my bum. "Git, girl, before I decide to keep you busy doing something else."

"Hmm. I like the sound of that."

"Git, I said," he chuckled.

When we entered the restaurant, the same maître d was there. He recognized me and bowed slightly. "Welcome back, my lady."

"Thank you. We're here to meet Coyote."

"Ah, yes. Right this way, please. He called to say he'd be a few minutes late and to please order yourselves a drink. He'll be here soon."

He led us to a front and center table, making it impossible for anyone to miss us as they entered or left. Being exposed like that made me uncomfortable, but I didn't say anything as Mike held our chairs, and Karen and I settled in. We ordered glasses of wine and relaxed with the background music that was soft and seductive. As we sat chatting, I felt prickles all along my spine. I looked to the entrance and found myself eye-to-eye with Johnny, my former boss from the Purple Passion Lounge. He was as surprised to see me as I was to see him. He hesitated, and I thought he seemed unsure whether to acknowledge me. As he stood there, he was gently pushed forward by several people behind him, leaving him no choice but to come forward.

When he got close to us, he nodded at me and then paused to ask, "What are you doing here?"

"Just visiting, Johnny. And you? What are you doing here?"

"The same," he said in a strained manner.

"Oh," I said. Then a thought came to me as he started forward. I called after him, "Are you still living in Las Vegas?"

He turned around. "But, of course…."

Mike and I looked at each other, perplexed. The Purple Passion Lounge was closed, so what was he up to? Why was he here? Earlier, Coyote had brought up the connection between Santa Fe and Las Vegas and their involvement in human trafficking. Did he know Isabella was here with Mike and me? Worry began to grow inside me. Was he here to reclaim her? I wouldn't put it past him. I was so lost in thought that I missed seeing Coyote approach our table.

Coyote shook Mike's hand, kissed me on the cheek, and then turned his full attention to Karen. Once again, Coyote spoke in Tewa, causing Karen to laugh. When I looked at her pink cheeks, she turned to me, answering my unspoken question. "Instead of saying, 'You are as beautiful as the rising sun,' he said, 'You are as beautiful as the setting sun.'"

I smiled at their flirting.

When his drink arrived, Coyote stood and lifted his glass. "Here's to the two most beautiful women in Santa Fe."

At his showy proclamation, we drew curious looks from the others in the restaurant. That made me more uncomfortable because I didn't want to attract Johnny's attention. I looked at Coyote and spoke softly, "Remember my telling you about seeing my former boss at the airport? Well, he's right in this restaurant sitting across from us. He's the one with the funny hairstyle. Do you see him?"

Coyote casually surveyed the room, and when he turned back to me, he said, "Thanks, Rosie. I'll look him up when I get to the office. What's his name again?"

"Johnny Cardoza," I said.

"No worries. I'll follow through. Now, ladies and kind sir, what is your pleasure tonight?"

Dinner was a joy, with good food, fine wine, and exciting conversation. It turned out that Coyote was a great storyteller. He talked a lot about growing up at the Tesuque Pueblo when his grandfather was the chief of their small tribe, and he was forced to learn the Indian ways. The rest of us remained quiet, entranced with his tales.

"Where did you go to school?" asked Karen, curious about education at the Pueblo.

"In the beginning, Grandmother taught my sister and me before we attended the Indian school in Tesuque. Of course, when I got older, I went to high school in Santa Fe," he said with a frown. "That was not an easy time, but I was lucky. A great teacher taught me that being rebellious was not the right way to succeed. She's the one who encouraged me to get into law enforcement—the best advice I ever got. What about you?"

Karen told Coyote about her early grade school years at a school around the corner from where she lived. Interestingly, she didn't mention her high school years, which had been trying for her. Instead, she went right into her time at Cornell, bringing me into the conversation. Nothing was said about her disastrous relationship with the stalker. I told some stories about our time there and turned to Karen with a smile, "Yup," I agreed. "True sister-friends."

Karen asked, "Is there any way for me to see the schools at the Pueblo? I'm always interested in seeing how other communities set up their schools."

"Thinking of teaching there?" Coyote asked with interest.

Karen blushed, unaware of how her question had left that thought open. "No, just curious," she answered, not wanting to make more of it than what it was.

"I'm sure we can figure something out," he responded. We heard voices raised and looked to the table where Johnny sat. There was a disagreement among the three who sat there. In a loud hushed whisper, I heard one of them say something about "territory" as he slapped his hand hard on the table. I looked at Mike, who flashed me a look, letting me know he'd also heard that part of the conversation.

All three men rose from their table and headed our way since it was the only way out of the restaurant. As Johnny passed our table, he looked at me with displeasure, and the other two men did the same. What was that about? Then the thought crossed my mind of how I'd ruined his scheme of auctioning the little girls off at the Purple Passion Lounge. Were those gentlemen part of that, too?

"You don't suppose they are here for Isabella, do you?" I asked as fear gripped me.

"I can't imagine Johnny would want to get involved with the same girl he must've been accused of taking, do you think?" answered Coyote in a calming voice.

"No, I guess not. I don't trust him, is all…."

Mike grabbed my hand and squeezed it hard. "I won't let anything happen to you or Isabella."

"I'll see what I can dig up. The mayor isn't too happy with the number of foreigners coming into our city and the recent murders that have occurred because of it. So the last thing we need here is another murder or any missing children," said Coyote.

"Amen," I said in agreement.

Coyote and Mike paid the bill. Then, we left the restaurant to stand in front of the building and wait for the valet to bring our car around. Coyote had come from the mayor's office on foot and would walk back to the police station nearby. He tipped his hat in the old western way and bent to leave me a perfunctory kiss on the cheek before pulling Karen closer, giving her a more intimate one. Then he jogged down the steps, and we watched him go.

"There is one heck of a cowboy. What do you think, Karen?" I asked.

"Oh my, yes! He sure is." She looked happy and as satisfied as I'd ever seen her. There was no doubt Coyote was sweeping her off her feet. At the moment, I didn't think her boyfriend stood a chance.

Mike looked at the two of us and shook his head.

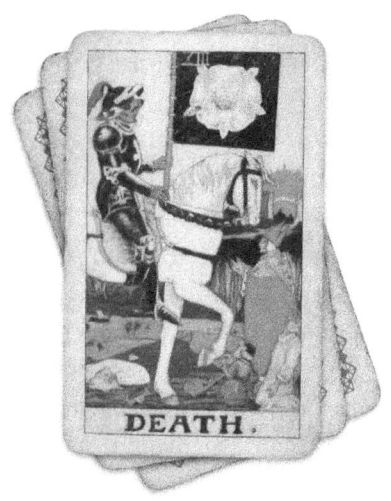

CHAPTER 18

T hanksgiving Day was a beautiful fall day, bright with sunshine and a cloudless sky. Mike had the football game on, cheering for the New England Patriots, while Isabella, Karen, and I completed last-minute tasks to ensure all was set for the holiday meal. I was excited to be the one hosting the dinner and a little nervous about it. I'd never fed that many people at one time before, and I wanted everything to go smoothly.

I was worried about seeing Miguel again after the fiasco of him paying to have dead crows placed at my door to scare me away from Isabella and Santa Fe. That'd ended up with him signed into an Anger Management course and seeing a counselor for six months. He'd not been pleased, but he'd brought it upon himself. He was Isabella's biological uncle and didn't want anyone to interfere with his 'owning' her. Unfortunately for him, what was best for Isabella was what

Maria and I agreed to do—raise her together. We had her mother's blessing, and things were going smoothly so far. Maybe not what Miguel wanted, but it was the way it was.

Little running feet were the first sign of their arrival. I'd removed anything too tempting for little hands and had a small table edged into the kitchen area with coloring books and other things I thought the boys might like to do. In Las Vegas, I'd bought several educational child iPad-type toys. An experiment on my part because I knew next to nothing about what little boys liked.

I opened the door to Angela, wearing a colorful dress that suited her. She was gaining more confidence, which showed in her smile. She held out the baby to me, and I reached for her. I lifted her into my arms and immediately began to talk baby talk, making Maria smile. Rosa, named for me, smiled wide, and I saw several new teeth. Maria held several casseroles in her arms—the Chili Relleno and tacos she'd promised to bring. Miguel stood behind her with the three little boys gathered around him.

"C'mon in, everyone!" I said, pointedly smiling at Miguel. He didn't return my smile but pushed the boys forward. My heart fell. So that is how it was going to be then.

Mike stood by my side and shook Miguel's hand when he entered. To break the ice, he asked. "How about a cold one?"

Miguel tipped his head in agreement, and when Mike returned, he held two beers—one for Miguel and one for himself. They sat to watch the game, not saying much.

The boys raced around and began chatting in Spanish when they saw the table I'd set up for them. Karen removed the casseroles from Maria, allowing her to calm the boys down and settle them at the table. Isabella and Angela had taken off to her bedroom. I looked around, pleased with all the activity. I still held the sleepy baby in my arms and watched as she closed her eyes. Looking at her, I wondered what it would be like to have a child of my own.

Once Rosa was put down for a nap and the boys were settled, I asked the ladies, "How about a glass of wine to celebrate the holiday?"

They nodded in agreement.

"How is the addition going, Maria?" I asked as I handed her a glass of Chardonnay.

"It's getting there. There are so many choices to make!"

"It's going to be lovely. I know the girls are excited about having your old bedroom as theirs."

The boys began to get rowdy, and Karen left and headed to their table. As a first-grade teacher, she wanted to see what they were doing. I turned to Maria, "Miguel doesn't seem too happy. Is everything okay?"

"I think he's embarrassed about what happened."

"He's not still upset with you, is he?"

"I think with the counselor's help, he's getting past that."

"Let's hope so."

"Have you run across your former neighbor, the one who was so nasty?"

"No, not since they moved, thank God. That's what made us decide to add to the house—his absence. I understand the house has been sold, and a nice older couple bought it."

"It'll be interesting to meet them."

"Yes, we're hoping they like noisy, small boys," said Maria, laughing.

"Your boys are so cute; what's not to like?"

The men began to cheer in the living room as their team was ahead. We girls looked at each other and smiled.

101

Leave it to sports to bring our men closer together. We had years ahead of us, and they would only be joyous if we all could get along.

The turkey was done, and it was time to serve dinner. Karen, Maria, and I worked as a team to serve buffet-style plates and get everyone but Rosa to the table. After we sat down, I asked, "Is everyone up for going around the table and saying what we're grateful for?"

The girls responded right away. The little boys' faces lit up after their mother helped them understand what I'd asked. "I want to!" said Armando, the oldest. The two younger boys shouted, "Me too!"

We chuckled, and even Miguel smiled.

"Okay, we'll go around the table, and I'll be last," I instructed.

Isabella and Angela were first. They'd been whispering together, and they looked at each other as they held clasped hands high in a sign of victory and said in unison. "We're glad we're sister-friends."

Maria and I looked at each other pleased. Then she said, "I'm grateful for my family, which now includes Isabella, Rosie, and Mike."

Mike's turn was next. "I'm grateful to my partner, Brian, for introducing me to Rosie and all it has brought about, including those sitting around the table."

The little boys were next. Armando began, "I'm..." 'grateful' Maria coached "for mama, papa, and...Angela and Rosa, and...and...trees outside, and...and...my toys, and...and...Santa Claus, and...tacos!"

"That was nice, Armando. What about you, Riccardo, and Miguel? What do you like?" asked Maria.

Riccardo laughed. "Tacos!"

"Me too," said little Miguel.

We laughed. Miguel was next and said simply, "I'm grateful for my family."

Then it was Karen's turn. "I like tacos, too, so that you know. But I'm grateful for the opportunity to spend time with my sister-friend and all of you this Thanksgiving holiday."

Then all eyes turned to me. My eyes filled. "Not long ago, most of my life consisted of Sweet Pea and me. And now, as I look around the table and see some of the people who've come into my life recently—my darling Isabella; Mike, the love of my life; and my new sister-friend Maria—I know how loved and blessed I am. I'm grateful to have each of you sitting at the table in my new life, and that means you too, Miguel. And, of course, my oldest friend, Karen."

All was quiet until Armando turned to his mother and questioned, "Why is she crying?"

"Because she's happy," answered Maria, patting him on the shoulder.

"Oh," said Armando, not understanding.

"Who would like some turkey?" asked Mike, standing at the head of the table with a carving knife hovering over the roasted bird before him. Earlier, we'd served up the rest of the meal in the kitchen, so only the turkey remained to be parceled out.

As we finished our meal, Rosa woke up demanding to be changed and fed. With full stomachs, we all had mellowed out, including the little boys who played quietly at the table with the games I'd bought. The guys watched another football game, not caring who won or not. Isabella and Angela were in Isabella's bedroom on the phone with Nica, who was going to be with them the next day at our house for the sleepover they'd planned.

We ended the day with sleepy little boys dragging their new games with them. After I closed the door on the last of them, I breathed a sigh of relief. The day had gone well, and I was pleased.

Mike left us to call Brian while Isabella got ready for bed. Karen and I remained in the kitchen.

"I can't believe how good I feel just being here in Santa Fe. I can honestly say I think I'd be happy living here."

I looked at her and raised my brows. "Really?"

"Yes. Besides, what do I have to lose by changing my life? It'd be a huge one for me, but...."

"What about your boyfriend?" I interrupted.

"It's never going to work, Rosie. For once, I don't feel obligated to stay in a relationship simply because someone likes me."

"I'm glad to see you take that stand. What would you do here then, Karen, teach?"

"That's what I'd love to do for sure." She paused deep in thought. "Maybe tomorrow I can look around some more, and that'll help me decide if this is where I want to live. No matter what I choose, I must clean up things with my boyfriend back in Boston."

"A move like this can be scary, huh? Does Coyote have anything to do with your wanting to change your plans?" I teased.

Karen's face turned crimson. "I think he's one fine cowboy, but I'm not considering getting into another relationship yet. No, Rosie, it's about the way this area makes me feel. It's hard to explain. I feel like I'm part of the earth here. Odd, isn't it?"

I thought about what she'd said. "Not really, Karen. It's not that odd. There's always a pull when your soul is part of a place. Don't you agree?"

"Yes. I need to move my life in a different direction, but I don't want to leap off the cliff," she laughed. "I'll keep my condo and perhaps just rent a place here for a while."

I saw Isabella coming toward us and turned to Karen. "It'll work out the way it's supposed to. You know that."

CHAPTER 19

T he following day, Karen received a telephone call from Coyote asking her if she'd like to see Tesuque Pueblo, where he lived and where one of the schools he attended was located. She hurriedly got dressed, face glowing as she waited for him to pick her up.

Love was in the air! Virginia and Cal in Las Vegas, and now Karen and Coyote in Santa Fe! Who knew? Now that Mike was in my life, it was hard to imagine that there wasn't a special someone for everyone. I shook my head at myself for making that thought seem so trite. For two people to find each other and be in a happy, healthy relationship was anything but that, and I was grateful for the blessing it was for me to have Mike in my life.

Mike sat at his computer, researching information on specific sites about missing girls in Nevada during the

107

past two years. I'd been involved in doing just that when I tried to identify the bones dumped at the job site, but it'd been four and five years ago, so my research was useless to him. Mike believed his client had been missing for less than a year, and his inability to learn more about her was frustrating. He wondered if she were still alive, perhaps living under a different name.

Isabella sat with me in the kitchen, sipping cocoa. "What are we going to serve for dinner tonight, Mama?"

"What would you like to serve?"

Grinning, she replied, "Pizza."

"No surprise there. You sure do love pizza, don't you? Well, it's all right with me as long as you have a green salad to go with it."

"Deal," she said as she got up and raced into her bedroom to answer her phone.

I continued sitting at the table, listing everything I wanted to complete before we returned for Christmas. I'd asked Virginia and Cal if they wanted to join us for a holiday here in Santa Fe, but I hadn't heard back yet. I wondered if Karen would like to come for Christmas. I wasn't sure how this would work out, but I wouldn't worry about it. I'd roll with it—no matter how it played out.

"Mama, can we pick up Nica now?"

"Sure. Let me get dressed, and we'll head out."

A knock on the door sounded—Coyote. Karen came hurrying to let him in, and a smile split his face when he saw her standing there. It was intriguing to see the obvious connection between Karen and Coyote. They looked good together with matching dark hair and brown eyes.

"Good morning, Coyote. Can I interest you in a cup of coffee?" I called out.

A glance at Karen and he answered, "No, thank you. We'll get coffee at the Pueblo."

"Before you leave, would you care to join us for dinner here tonight, Coyote?"

A second look at Karen. "That'd be great."

"How about six o'clock then?"

"Sounds good; I'll bring some wine."

"Okay, then. Have a good time, you two," I said as Karen and Coyote turned toward each other and smiled.

"See you later," said Karen, grabbing Coyote's arm and heading out.

A short while later, Isabella and I arrived at the Palace of the Governors to pick up Nica. Nica was sitting next to Grandmother, who was napping, and she rose to greet us as we walked their way. Isabella raced forward, and the two girls squealed and hugged each other. That was enough to wake Grandmother.

"Hello, my daughter. Come near," she called, fluttering her hand.

I bent to kiss her cheeks. "My, you're cold. Here let me wrap your shawl tighter around you."

She reached for my hand. "Help me up. I'm going inside. It's too cold for me here. Nica's mother is driving me back to the pueblo at noon."

"Why don't we all go next door to the restaurant, and I'll get us something hot to drink? Then we'll go pick up Angela. Is that alright with you, girls?"

I steadied myself as I hefted Grandmother to her feet, and we headed to the nearby restaurant. We sat around a small table near the window, and when I looked outside, I nearly choked on my coffee. Was that Maria's former neighbor I saw?

"What is wrong, my daughter?" asked Grandmother.

"I must be seeing things. I thought I saw Maria's former neighbor pass by. I knew they'd moved, but I should've known they wouldn't move far away from Santa Fe. I'm sure Coyote wouldn't have allowed that with his court case looming."

Grandmother was quiet. Then she covered my hand with hers. "There's more danger ahead for you, my daughter."

That was the last thing I wanted to hear, and I said with some irritation, "That's not anything I wanted to hear."

She shrugged an apology. I exhaled and calmed myself. Even though I'd have to be on guard, I wouldn't let anything lock me into a state of fear. I sighed. I didn't know if I'd share Grandmother's warning with Mike. After all, he couldn't do anything about it and had enough on his mind.

"Mama, we're going to be late to pick up Angela!" cried Isabella with her arm around Nica.

Grandmother patted my hand. "Go. I'm going to sit here where it's warm. Nica's mother will be here in a few minutes."

We kissed Grandmother, and before I could leave, she grabbed my hand and pulled me back. "I love you, my daughter."

"And I love you too, my mother," I told my mother from a previous lifetime.

As I pulled into Maria's house, the rooftop and studs of the new addition stood out. It looked huge. The girls raced to meet Angela, and I followed close behind. Maria met us at the door with the baby in her arms. "Do you want to see the addition?" she asked as she handed the baby to me.

I stepped into the opening via what used to be Maria's closet. It was easy to see that a double bathroom would be installed so that the girls would have their own bathroom in addition to the one in the master bedroom space. How nice! The new addition would be beautiful and add value to the house. Maria's eyes glowed with excitement as she pointed out where she planned to put things.

"I worried about keeping the three boys together in one room, but they didn't want to be separated when I spoke to the two older ones. Since their bedroom is the same size as our old bedroom, I think they'll be okay … at least for now. Boys aren't as fussy as girls. Thank God for that."

I smiled. "It's going to be beautiful, Maria."

"Yes, I think so too. Do you have time for tea?"

The girls decided for us. "Mama, we're ready to go!"

I kissed the baby's neck as she grabbed my hair. I released her grip and kissed her fingers before handing her back to Maria. "Next time, okay?"

Maria set Rosa on her hip. "Angela, be good and have fun."

"Yeess, Mama. Come on, let's go."

"You girls, go ahead. I want to pop in and say hello and goodbye to the boys."

When I opened their bedroom door, I was amazed at all the toys strung across the floor and all three beds. There was no room to walk, so I stood at the doorway and raised my voice against their arguing. "Hi, guys! I wanted to say hello and goodbye."

They jumped up and came forward. "Where are you going?" Armando asked. "You just got here."

Ahh, the pragmatic one, I thought. I turned to Maria, and we shared the same thought. "I know, but I didn't want to miss seeing you, guys."

"Okay, goodbye," Armando said, accepting me at my word.

"Goodbye," echoed Ricardo and little Miguel.

I chuckled to myself. Yup, little boys were very different from little girls.

CHAPTER 20

T he girls were like magpies chattering in the car's back seat. When we arrived home, Sweet Pea raced from one to the other to get as much attention as possible. She considered herself one of them and hung around them wherever they stepped. All three girls included her as if she were one of them. I laughed while watching them.

Mike came up behind me and put his arms around me. "What are you laughing at?" he whispered, tightening his grip on me.

"I'm just happy," I responded.

He kissed me. "What's for lunch?"

"Turkey sandwiches. The girls want pizza tonight, and I thought I'd pick up a steak for us adults. Coyote is going to join us."

"Nice. Extra testosterone," Mike laughed.

"Like you need it, handsome," I teased. "C'mon. Help me make the sandwiches for the girls too."

After cleaning up, I left Mike with the girls and drove off to Albertson's to get a steak and enough fresh greens for a salad for the girls and our dinner. I parked my car and headed into the store. The memories of the deaths that'd taken place there surrounded me and made me shiver. Shaking off those thoughts, I entered the store and became enchanted with all the Christmas decorations displayed. I joined in the upbeat nature of the other shoppers wrapped up in the holiday spirit, and I placed a rosemary bush shaped like a Christmas tree into my shopping cart. Christmas was going to be special this year by sharing it with many people I loved.

When I arrived home, I called out, "Anyone home?" as I came through the door carrying a large grocery bag.

Isabella, Nica, and Angela came running. "Oh, what beautiful flowers!"

"Those are my favorite," said Nica. "I love sunflowers. They're good to eat!"

"Good to eat? Really?" asked Isabella.

Nica laughed. "Yes, the seeds are."

"Cool," said Isabella.

Later, I ordered the pizza for the girls and sat with them for a few minutes to make sure they each had a salad to go with their meal. Then I left them whispering and giggling, enjoying their time together. My heart was happy.

Soon, Coyote and Karen blew in, cheeks rosy and eyes bright. What a handsome couple, I thought as I studied them. "Welcome back!" I said.

Coyote handed Mike the wine he'd brought, and they both went to the kitchen counter to uncork it. Karen smiled.

"I'm going to wash my face and fix my hair. I'll be right back."

Karen stopped at the table where the girls were eating, and they laughed at something she said. The girls finished up and went into Isabella's room while we gathered around the kitchen bar area, sipping our wine and nibbling the appetizers I'd set out.

After a silence, Mike asked, "So Karen, how's school going?"

The conversation turned to schools in general and how difficult it had become for a teacher to teach. Instead, a teacher was under pressure to comply with the school regulations that required children to learn enough to be tested on specific studies. Karen explained, "This leaves little time to do much more to expand their minds beyond what is required."

Coyote spoke up. "That's why I'm grateful for the schools at the Pueblo, where they have required classes to learn some of the old Indian ways. Nica is still involved in those classes, and I'm glad she is. She's come to appreciate much more about all that surrounds her—especially gifts from Mother Nature."

"Like what, specifically?" Karen asked.

"See that desert plant down the hill; it's a special healing plant. Come, I'll show you," Coyote said as he pulled her up from her seat and led her down to it.

I looked at Mike and said, "Why don't you help me set things out for the grill? We'll get dinner started, okay?"

Mike smiled. "Want to leave the love birds alone, do you?"

"Whatever gave you that idea?" I teased.

The girls came skipping out to the kitchen. They held up several decorated pieces of paper with our names printed on them. They used stickers to complete the place cards they'd made. They set them on the dining room table, placing a card at each spot.

"C'mon, Mama and Mike, come look!" demanded Isabella.

We bent over the first one placed at the head of the table. The card had my name on it with a sticker of an Eagle, and its meaning printed in small letters: *divine spirit, connection to the creator*. Next came Mike's with a label of an elk. Its meaning was *strength, agility, and freedom*. I had to smile at the word freedom because that was a side of Mike I knew existed. "Oh, my! These are so interesting!" I said, taking in their excitement.

Mike stood and stared at his place card and nodded in agreement. He looked at Isabella and smiled. She grinned. "Here, Mama, these are for Coyote and Aunt Karen."

I was curious to see what spirit animals the girls had chosen for them. Coyote's sticker was of a cougar, meaning *leadership and courage*. Karen's sticker was of a deer, meaning *love, goodness, and kindness*. An excellent choice for her, I thought. I knew she'd be pleased to have the girls see her that way.

"What about your place cards? Did you make up any for yourself?" I asked.

Angela shyly brought her hand from behind her back and held up three. She handed them to me. I looked at each one. "They're all the same!"

The girls giggled. "What are these?" I asked as I could barely make out hand-drawn angel wings.

The girls giggled again. Then Nica proudly said, "Those are angel wings, Rosie! Grandmother always calls us little angels, so that's what we are. We looked it up. It said it means *guardians of hope and wonder*."

"How did you girls come up with this?" I asked.

Nica answered. "That's what they teach us at the Pueblo—all about the animal spirits."

"Pretty cool, huh?" Isabella said with pride.

As Karen and Coyote approached with their hands intertwined, she called out, "C'mon and check out your place cards!"

The girls gathered around them and began their showing.

I stepped back into the kitchen to carry out the platter of beef tenderloins and handed it to Mike, who stood ready at the grill. "Eight minutes on the first side, flip, and 5 minutes on the second side, please ... should be perfect."

The meal was fabulous, and all things flowed—a perfect evening. When it was close to 9 o'clock, Coyote looked at his watch. "What time is your flight tomorrow, Karen?"

"One o'clock."

"If you like, I can drive you to the airport."

Karen flushed and looked at me. I nodded. "Sure, I'd like that," she said.

"Okay, then. I'll pick you up at around ten o'clock. Is that okay?" Coyote asked as he rose from his seat to say goodnight.

Karen walked Coyote to his car and re-entered the house with scarlet cheeks. "Oh, my," she said and plopped on the couch beside me. We clasped hands like schoolgirls and relaxed together for a few minutes. Then we each headed to bed, ready for a good night's sleep.

CHAPTER 21

T he following day, I untangled myself from Mike's arms wrapped around me and lightly kissed his cheek. He didn't stir. I followed the scent of coffee into the kitchen to see Karen sitting at the table, sipping from a steaming mug. She smiled when she saw me. Karen got up to pour me a cup of coffee, returned, and sat beside me. She had something on her mind, although she was reluctant to bring it to my attention.

"Karen, would you like to join us here for Christmas?"

She was startled, knowing I'd read her mind. "Would that be okay?"

"Not only okay but delightful. Our other sister-friends already have plans, and sharing the holiday with you would be wonderful. Isabella, Mike, and all the rest of the family would enjoy that. And we know Coyote would for sure," I chuckled.

"It'd be so much easier not to be in Boston with my boyfriend there." She paused. "Soon-to-be, ex-boyfriend."

"I get it. No worries."

We looked at each other and smiled when we heard the girls giggling. Soon they marched into the kitchen. "Where's Mike?" asked Isabella.

Since Mike was usually the first up in the morning, it seemed odd not to have him here starting breakfast. "Maybe you should get him up," I said.

The girls squealed and raced into our bedroom just as he stepped out. "Hey, what's going on?" he asked as he saw the girls jumping around.

"We came to get you up," said Isabella.

"You did, did you?" he said, hugging her.

"Yup. We're hungry!" said Nica.

Mike laughed. "Okay, girls. Let me go, and I'll start breakfast. Who wants pancakes?"

"We do!" the girls hollered.

The morning flew by. We said goodbye to Karen, made much easier by knowing she'd be returning for Christmas. After lunch, we dropped Nica off with her mother at the museum where she worked and Angela back home. Our flight back to Las Vegas was in the morning, so we didn't have much time to do all I wanted to get done before we returned for Christmas.

Isabella's phone began ringing in her bedroom. "I'll get it!" she said. After a while, Isabella strolled into the kitchen. "Mama, guess what Tiffany said?"

"What, sweetheart?"

"Tiffany said when the chauffeur dropped her off today at the soup kitchen, she got to sit out front with the people eating there. She was told, 'There were too many cooks in the kitchen.' And one of the older men there told Tiffany she was so pretty she could be a movie star, and he would help her."

The image of the two men I'd worried over when I'd seen them at the soup kitchen flashed across my mind. "I'm not sure I like the sound of that."

"Why not, Mama?"

"Men sometimes say things to flatter, and that's not their real intention."

"What do you mean? Don't you think Tiffany is pretty enough?"

"Of course I do. It's just that you have to be careful around people you don't know and trust. Sometimes if they give you compliments, it's so that you will like them or do something for them that isn't always good. Kinda like what you've been through."

She thought it over. "You mean they aren't always truthful?"

"Yes, that's exactly what I mean. Is Tiffany still at the soup kitchen?"

"No, her chauffeur picked her up and took her back to her house."

"Good." I thought it unusual that Tiffany would be out front eating with the guests, but then maybe she'd caused enough trouble in the kitchen that they had no choice but to put her there. There was no question that with Tiffany around, it was a worry.

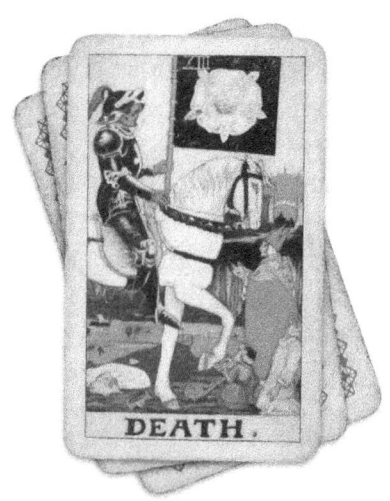

CHAPTER 22

I f you didn't count the crowds of people that we had to push through to reach our bags and make it out to the parking garage, our flight home was uneventful. Mike had left his car there, and we eagerly climbed into it, excited to be home.

Virginia had left me a note saying she had prepared a chicken casserole in the freezer to take out when I wanted. I'd pop it into the oven when it was time for dinner. Thank God for her saving the day for me. I climbed the stairs, unpacked, and gathered the dirty clothes from all our suitcases. I carried them down the hall to the laundry room located at the end, past all the bedrooms.

As I went through the pockets of the clothes before I tossed them into the washer, I felt a crumpled piece of paper in Mike's pants pocket. I reached in and pulled it out. I unraveled it to find a receipt from a jewelry store in

Santa Fe with nothing but his name and a pickup date of 12/24. I threw it on top of the loose change he'd laid upon his dresser. I couldn't imagine what it was for unless his watch was being repaired.

I went downstairs with the list I had drawn up in Santa Fe for all I'd need to do to be organized for the Christmas holiday season. I had a lot to do, especially since it'd be our first time in Santa Fe for Christmas.

Isabella came into the office. "Tiffany wants to know if she can come over."

"Not tonight. Maybe tomorrow night, if it's okay with her parents."

"I'll tell her, although I don't think she will like it."

"Isabella? She doesn't have to like it," I snapped. "It's just the way it's going to be. Besides, she'll see you in school tomorrow, only a few hours away."

"Okay, Mama. It's no big deal."

I couldn't stop myself from snapping at anything concerning Tiffany. After Isabella left, Sweet Pea stayed behind and put her paws on my knees, sensing I was out of sorts. I lifted her and snuggled her under my chin. "It's okay, little girl. I'm just grumpy, is all. A good night's sleep will take care of that. Are you getting hungry? Come on, and I'll fix your dinner."

I placed Sweet Pea on the floor and watched her twirling in excitement. I laughed at her antics and began to feel better. She was such a good dog, and I was happy she'd taken to Isabella, who seemed to love her as much as I did.

Later, we all seemed distracted and went through the motions of doing what we needed to do without any enthusiasm. I wasn't the only one who was tired.

That night, I curled up next to Mike and breathed in his scent—outdoorsy with a touch of pine. He heard my sniffing him and laughed. "What are you doing?"

"Smelling the essence of you," I said. "You smell like the woods on Mt. Charleston."

"Well, I can guarantee you I haven't been there lately, or you would have been with me." He flipped over to face me and nuzzled my neck. "And you smell good enough to eat!"

That was all it took for me to forget how tired I was. After our lovemaking, I snuggled against Mike, satisfied and relaxed enough to let any worries dissipate into a dreamless sleep. I never stirred until daylight streamed through the shutters the following day. I awoke refreshed and grateful for the whole night's undisturbed sleep. Ah, another beautiful day.

I got ready to go to the construction site after sending Isabella to school with extra hugs and kisses. Mike kissed me goodbye and headed down to the office. He had received applications to review for the office position he had posted, and he wanted my opinion on them. He asked if I'd meet him at the office after I ensured all was okay at the site.

When I pulled onto the construction site, I startled Butch, who was talking to Tony. I marched forward, upset to see them there together. "What are you doing here, Tony?"

"Haven't you heard? I'm building a new place around the corner from here. Butch is going to be my contractor."

"Not until he's finished here," I countered.

"Well, I'm afraid I have some bad news for you then."

"What do you mean?" I asked, alarmed.

"I've just hired him for more money than he can ever make where he is now."

I turned to Butch. "Really?"

He nodded with a smug smile. "Yup, this is my last day."

"Why, Tony? Why are you doing this?" I asked. "You won't be ready for him until the foundation is in."

"I don't have to justify my reasons to you."

A thought occurred to me. "Is Johnny going to be working with you?"

Tony was startled, surprised I'd asked. "What is it to you?"

"Ahh. Back to your old tricks, then."

"Whaddya mean by that?"

I walked away, disgusted. I texted Mimi. "Do you know what Tony is up to?"

Immediately, I received a text back. "I just found out. Let's meet."

"On my way. Let Romano know."

I called Mike and told him what had happened. "That confuses things, but it's not a big deal or shouldn't be. Just be sure you approve of who the contractor puts in charge."

"Let's hope it's someone honest. Please check our contract to see what it says about the contractor's obligations. There's something in it where we can demand the site manager see the construction through to the end."

"I think you might be right; however, that doesn't make for a happy employee if he doesn't want to be there. And that's a problem."

"I agree, but I think that gives us some wiggle room for getting the new site manager we want."

"Ahh. Good thinking. I'll check. Are you meeting with Mimi and Romano now?"

"Yes, then I'll join you until it's time for Isabella to come home from school. She's bringing Tiffany with her, and I want to be sure to be there."

"Good idea," agreed Mike.

The meeting went well. We called our contractor, who, after listening to us, said, "I'll send Eddie to you. He's the best site manager I have."

"Really?" Mimi snapped. "Then why wasn't he on our job to begin with?"

I left Mimi's after we agreed to meet the general contractor and the new site manager first thing in the morning with the contractor's promise, "You'll like him."

I headed to Mike's office. When I entered, he was talking to a prospective client. "Yes, we can take care of that. No worries. If you send me the information, I'll review it and get back to you with a proposal."

As a sign of success, I raised my thumb and placed one of the two specialty coffees I'd picked up for us on his desk.

I went to the receptionist's desk out front and shuffled through the applications. Several of them had photos, which surprised me. One picture on the top of the pile drew my attention. With so many people competing for a single position, were those who were attractive enough using their looks to get a foot in the door?

A stunning and slightly familiar face looked out in all her beauty. I closed my eyes and tried to picture where I'd seen her before. Yes, that was it! She had been one of the newer dancers at the Purple Passion Lounge. She'd be nothing but trouble here, I thought. I hoped Mike knew better than to fall for her as his secretary. I picked up the application and shoved it into the back of the pile when I heard Mike behind me ask, "Why did you do that, Rosie?"

My face burned. "That girl would be nothing but trouble here."

"Says who, Ms. Smarty Pants?"

"You're not serious, are you, Mike?"

"She's due here any minute for an interview."

"You're kidding, right?"

"Don't you recognize her? She used to work at the Purple Passion Lounge, and I thought if I interviewed her, I might be able to find out if she's still in contact with the other girls or Johnny."

"You're not going to hire her, are you?"

Mike stood and smiled at me. "You're not jealous, are you?" He came and put his arms around me. "I'd never hire her for any position here. You ought to know better than that, my worried friend."

We both jumped at the knock on the door. I smiled at Mike and thought, had I been a bit jealous? Shame on me. When Annette came through the door, she brought back memories of my working at the Purple Passion Lounge … not all that pleasant. She eyed me, and I knew she wondered why I was there for the interview. I let Mike handle it and sat to the side as an observer. Seeing him in his professional role was interesting because he was so formal and not the Mike I knew. I realized his being closed off to them was an enticement sometimes for women to want to "change" that demeanor—a challenge of sorts.

Mike turned to me several times and said, "Isn't that right, Rosie?"

I nodded and smiled. "That's right."

I winked at him when he looked puzzled at my lack of response. I knew Annette wouldn't be as responsive to his questions if I had taken a more significant part in the interview. A girl thing.

After she left, I said to Mike, "That went fairly well. We learned she knew Tony was renovating another site, and she'd probably work for him when it opened. At least she'd been honest when she said she was looking for something to hold her over until then. She also saw Johnny talking with Tony when she went there the other day, which confirms they will be working together."

"True, but I still need someone to run this place.

Are you sure you can't give me a hand here?"

"Only when you're in a jam, handsome. Here, let me go through these applications again. You need an older woman with experience and one you can trust."

"Okay, you look. I've got to put in a call to Brian to discuss this new client."

I picked out an application, and it felt warm all over. I read through it and took it to Mike. "Here she is! Patricia Newheart."

"Seriously?"

"Yup, call her right now. I think she'll be available later this afternoon."

He studied me. "Okay, hand it over, and I'll call her."

I went to the front and studied the painting on the wall. It was in the wrong location; I'd have Mike change it later. Once we hired a secretary, I'd bring live plants to spruce up the place. Until then, it'd be a waste of money because Mike had too much to do without watering the plants.

"Okay, she'll be here at 3 o'clock. Let's get some lunch, okay?" asked Mike as he approached the front.

"How does she sound?"

"Very pleasant."

"Good. I can't wait to hear how the interview goes."

"How about some Thai food? There's a restaurant right down the street from here."

"That's fine with me. I already know what I'm ordering."

"You do?"

"Yup. Their special—whatever it is."

"I love a brave woman," he laughed, grabbing my hand and pulling me along.

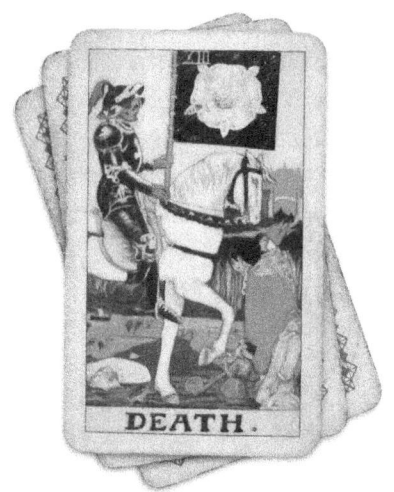

CHAPTER 23

I arrived home with plenty of time to be there when Isabella and Tiffany got home from school. I heard them before I saw them. They were arguing, and I was delighted to hear Isabella say, "I'm not going to ask, no matter how angry you get, Tiffany."

As Isabella became increasingly settled in as my "daughter," she was becoming secure in that role and no longer afraid to speak up and stand her ground when differences of opinion occurred. And I was happy that she was stepping into the role of a pre-teenager like any soon-to-be 12-year-old. Her birthday was in a few weeks, and I knew she wanted to celebrate it with her sister-friends in Santa Fe.

"Did you have a good day at school?" I asked after the girls had gotten settled at the kitchen table. Neither girl looked too happy.

"It was okay," Isabella said. "I got a C in Math today. The teacher says that'll change if I keep at it."

"Math is easy for me," boasted Tiffany. "I got an A."

"Oh, I didn't realize you two were in the same class," I said.

"We're not," responded Isabella, rolling her eyes.

Tiffany eyed Isabella provocatively. "Isabella said that she wanted to go shopping."

"No, I didn't, Tiffany."

"Well, I think that sounds like fun," she snapped. "Don't you agree, Rosie?"

I took in a deep breath to calm myself. I needed to remember that there were battles and wars. I let Tiffany calling me Rosie go. "I think that if there is something that you want, Tiffany, it should come from you and not by saying something that isn't true simply because it might work out better for you. Do you understand what I'm saying?"

Tiffany sat still for a minute, taking in what I'd said. "So, do you want to go shopping then?"

This time it was my turn to roll my eyes. "No, I don't, thank you. Why don't you girls get something cold to drink? We will have hotdogs tonight in honor of you, Tiffany, so maybe the two of you could bake some cookies for dessert. What do you think, Isabella?"

"Alright, I guess," she responded, picking up Sweet Pea and snuggling her in her lap.

"I'll decorate them!" squealed Tiffany. "You can help me, Isabella," she granted.

I left them to go into the office and begin another article for Living Well Magazine. I'd written one on patience the last time Tiffany had been there. I wondered if I could write about how to dismiss thoughts of murdering someone, but

I decided that wouldn't do. I thought about Tiffany and her obnoxious behavior. Weren't her parents aware that she would end up lonely if they didn't guide her to act differently? Tiffany couldn't be oblivious to the reaction of others, could she?

I wasn't happy that Isabella hadn't brought other kids home with her—especially those more her age. I'd have to encourage her to do so. It was essential for her to have people around her who were uplifting. Negative energy was not suitable for anyone's health.

Time slipped by, and soon Mike walked through the door, wearing a grin. "You were right, Rosie. That woman was dynamite."

"Wonderful!" I exclaimed. "What is she like?"

"A little bit like Irene next door. Not quite as old, but experienced in the corporate world. Patricia said she'd become bored after retirement and wanted to return to a regular job. We set her hours from 7:00 a.m. to 2:00 p.m. to coordinate with Brian's hours back east."

"I'm so glad. When will Patricia start?"

"Next Monday."

"You've got to be relieved."

"Yes, especially as we have more work coming in."

We heard Isabella's raised voice. "Tiffany, you have to take turns."

"But I'm the guest!" Tiffany cried out.

"If you want to stay in my house, you must share," warned Isabella.

"Okay, but you don't have to be so mean about it." Mike and I looked at each other and shook our heads.

He whispered, "Good for Isabella for standing up for herself."

I nodded and held my thumb up in victory.

"What's for dinner?" Mike asked.

I smiled. "You mean you're still hungry after all that Thai food? I bought some hotdogs for supper, especially for Tiffany, because she likes them so much, and I was hoping you'd be willing to grill them outside. I also bought a medley of vegetables to do as well."

"Sure. How about I pour us a glass of wine first?"

We sat in the living room in front of the fire. We relaxed as we listened to the girls in the kitchen laughing over something.

"That's sure a nicer sound, isn't it?" I asked.

"Yes... so much better than all that fussing."

Later, while Mike grilled the hotdogs, Tiffany and Isabella went outside to watch him. I glanced out and became alarmed as I saw Tiffany sidle close to Mike and hook her arm through his to get his attention. She flicked her long, blond hair over her shoulder and looked adoringly at him. I was more than a little irritated. I slid open the sliding glass door as Mike twisted his arm away from her grasp. He frowned and looked annoyed.

"Tiffany, stand back and let Mike do the grilling. Better yet, why don't you and Isabella come inside and set the table?"

"Good idea," Mike added.

Tiffany flounced inside, and Isabella followed with a look of apology. After they were inside, I tapped Tiffany on the shoulder. "That kind of behavior is not acceptable, Tiffany. Hear me?"

I was gratified to see Tiffany blush.

"I'm sorry, Mama," whispered Isabella as she passed me.

Dinner was tense. Even Tiffany was subdued. At the end of the meal, the girls passed around the cookies they'd made.

"Thank you for making the cookies, Isabella and Tiffany. They're delicious," I said.

"I think the ones with the pink icing are the best," announced Tiffany.

"Are those the ones that you decorated?" I asked, sure she had.

"Yup. They're the prettiest," Tiffany answered, flipping her hair back, eying Mike.

He immediately glanced away.

I was unhappy with Tiffany's behavior. "Why don't you girls excuse yourselves and go do your homework? I'll clean up the kitchen."

Isabella and Tiffany rose and left us. Interestingly enough, Sweet Pea didn't follow.

I turned to Mike. "I certainly am not going to put up with that behavior from Tiffany."

"I don't blame you. Do all teenage girls flirt like that?"

"Nooo, they don't. How would you feel if you saw Isabella behave like that?"

"Isabella? Oh, she'd never do that."

"You didn't answer my question. How would you feel if Isabella acted like Tiffany?"

Mike frowned. "You don't think I encouraged that, do you?"

"No, I don't. I'm pretty sure you'd be upset if Isabella acted that way, and I think you'd wonder why she needed to do that."

"So, what do you think is going on with Tiffany?"

"Tiffany is a beautiful young girl, and I think she's insecure enough to test out if she can use her beauty to get what she wants. I'm no psychiatrist; I'm just saying what I sense. So I think I'll discuss this with the therapist Isabella and I are seeing."

"Is it worth it for Isabella to keep Tiffany as a friend?" asked Mike.

"I dunno. I need to seek help because I'm unhappy about the situation. The only thing I know for sure is that Tiffany has trouble ahead."

After Tiffany left and Isabella was in bed, I went to sit with her, as was our habit of late. As soon as I sat beside her, Isabella said, "Mama, I know you're angry with Tiffany. She said she hadn't done anything wrong."

"Really? Why do you think I might be upset?"

She blushed. "She was acting like a 'la puta,'" she mumbled.

At first, I wasn't sure I'd heard Isabella correctly. Then my face flushed as I recognized the Spanish word for a slut, prostitute. La puta? "Yes, that's right."

"I think she just wants attention, Mama."

'I think you're right, but how she's going about it will get her in trouble. She doesn't seem to understand that she's crossed the line of decent behavior. Little girls shouldn't behave that way."

"I know."

"I want you to have less to do with Tiffany. It's time to expand your girlfriends to include other girls you like rather than feel sorry for. It's important to surround yourself with girls like your sister-friends—ones who are kind and trustworthy. Don't you agree?"

"What will I say to Tiffany?"

"You don't have to explain spending time with other friends. Meantime, you'll see her on Saturday, and you can tell her I'm happy to pick her up and drive her with us to the soup kitchen. Remind her to be on time, is all."

Isabella was thoughtful. "Okay, Mama."

"I love you, Isabella. I hope you understand that I want the best for you, and that includes wanting you to have friends who treat you nicely."

"I understand, Mama. I love you too."

As I walked away, my thoughts drifted. Young girls today seemed not to honor or respect their feminine role in loving ways. Instead, it was too easy for them to discount themselves by acting as someone with little pride and willing to flaunt themselves in front of any male. I was aware that these were tough times for a young girl. Through all the social media and peer pressure, everything seemed to set them up as competitors—who's the prettiest, smartest, thinnest, and more? Now with their increased sexual knowledge, it seemed to boil down to the number of notches on their belt of how many men they seduced. These are crazy times, for sure. What was going to happen to Tiffany?

CHAPTER 24

S aturday came, and once again, I sat outside in the car, waiting for Tiffany to join us for our volunteer work at the soup kitchen. Ten minutes later, the front door opened, and Isabella raced forward. Tiffany stumbled after her, pulling her jacket on, one sleeve at a time.

"Good morning, Tiffany," I greeted.

"Hi, Rosie," she grumbled.

"Tiffany, please call me Ms. Bennett. That's the polite way to address an adult."

She glared at me but didn't say a word. The ride to the soup kitchen was quiet, and I was glad to swing into the parking lot.

"C'mon," said Isabella as she grabbed hold of Tiffany to run inside.

"Don't pull on me!" Tiffany complained.

"Sorry," Isabella said.

Once inside, I donned an apron and lined up with the others to serve the food. The girls ran into the kitchen to join the other three girls and their mothers. It was colder outside than the last time I'd been there, and it was easy to see that some of our guests needed hats and mittens. Irene, our next-door neighbor, was always crocheting hats and mittens, donating them to her church. Maybe she'd give some of them here. I'd have to ask her.

We had nearly finished serving everyone when we heard a shrill scream from the kitchen. I dropped my serving spoon into the pan and ran to the back. "Don't, Tiffany! Don't hit her!" demanded Isabella, who was pulling on her.

A small girl cowered in the corner while Tiffany stood over her with a fist raised. Two mothers came forward and reached for Tiffany. "Stop!" I yelled.

My voice resounded, and all who stood there turned toward me. "Isabella and Tiffany, come with me! Out front, now!" I looked at the mothers, "We'll straighten this out after everyone is served."

They nodded, and one of the mothers said, "Back to work, girls."

I pushed the girls to a corner table in the front and demanded, "Sit there until I'm through serving, and don't move!"

Isabella's eyes filled, and it was easy to see she was mortified. Tiffany, on the other hand, simply looked sullen. I returned in line with a tight smile to the two other ladies serving the food. As I helped the last of the people, one of the two men I worried about being unstable walked to the table where the girls sat. He bent down and stroked Tiffany's hair and said something to her. She looked up and smiled and flicked her hair back, preening. I felt sick as I watched how easily she fell for what undoubtedly had been a compliment. I wanted to scream.

One of the other women serving turned to me, "Go ahead. We'll finish up here."

"Thanks," I said, grateful she'd understood my concern. As I walked toward the table, I tried not to overreact.

"Girls, let's go into the back."

The man stared first at me, then looked back and forth between the girls and me. "You, her mother? You don't look like her. She's prettier. So's the other one."

Tiffany smiled and preened. "She's definitely not my mother."

"Excuse us, please, sir. Come on, girls. Let's go." I urged.

"He's going to make me into a movie star," Tiffany bragged as she rose from her seat.

"We'll see about that," I muttered to myself. We entered the kitchen to face the smaller girl and her mother. I turned to Tiffany and Isabella. "So, what's the story here? What happened?"

Tiffany stood up straight. "She wouldn't let me have a turn at the stove," she accused.

"Is that true?" I asked Isabelle and the other girl.

"I hadn't finished my turn yet," said the small girl in a quavering voice. "I'd just begun."

The mother stepped forward and scowled at Tiffany. "You are a pushy, rude bully." She turned to me. "She always wants things her way, and each time she's been here, she's caused a problem. I don't think she's earned the right to be here."

"Tiffany, what do you have to say for yourself?" I asked.

"I have the right to be here if I want," she challenged. "I didn't do anything wrong."

I closed my eyes and inhaled deeply. There would be no apology coming from Tiffany. "Look, I'm sorry for this upset. I'm afraid it's not my decision whether Tiffany returns or not. You'll have to take that up with the school," I said.

"We certainly will," warned the mother as she grabbed her daughter's hand and marched away.

I sighed. "Tiffany, when will you ever learn?" As I glanced at her, I realized she'd gotten what she wanted—attention. It didn't seem to matter that it came from her negative behavior. "C'mon, let's go," I ordered.

We loaded into the car, not saying a word. As we drove along, all was quiet until Tiffany asked, "Why are you angry at me, *Mrs.* Bennett?"

"I'm not angry as much as I'm disappointed that your bad behavior continues to get you into trouble. Being you can't be fun when everyone around you becomes upset with you and your actions."

Our eyes locked, and, for once, Tiffany didn't have a retort. All three of us remained silent. When we arrived at Tiffany's house, she opened her car door, got out, and lurched toward her front door without turning back, waving… or even saying goodbye.

Isabella and I looked at each other, unhappy with how things had turned out.

CHAPTER 25

That night, Mike was in an upbeat mood. He'd stopped and picked up steaks for dinner and a special bottle of Pinot wine. "What's the occasion?" I asked.

"Since Isabella is spending the night with Gramma Irene next door, I thought I'd make this a date night—the two of us alone for a change."

"Hmm. I know something the two of us can do," I murmured as I snuggled into Mike's arms and kissed him.

The house phone rang, surprising both of us, and we reluctantly pulled apart. "I'll get it," I groaned.

"Hello?"

"Is this Rosalie Bennett?"

"Yes, it is. Who's calling, please?"

"This is Tiffany's mother calling, and I understand there was an issue this morning at the volunteer place."

"Yes, there certainly was...."

"Tiffany told me all about it. I understand that Isabella was involved too. I believe it's best that Tiffany no longer has anything to do with you and your *ward*. You are a bad influence on my daughter, and I don't want my daughter associating with your kind."

"What exactly did your daughter tell you?" I asked in a frosty tone.

"It doesn't matter. I'm asking you to please honor my request to keep the girls apart."

My face heated, and my heart pounded with fury. "You can count on it. You have my word. Goodbye," I ended in a clipped manner.

I lowered the phone with disbelief and returned to where Mike was sitting. "You're not going to believe what just happened."

Mike held his arm wide and said, "Come here and tell me all about it before you burst." He watched me as I moved closer to him on the couch. "Are those tears I see?"

I wiped my face. "I'm just so angry! And when I get this mad, sometimes tears come. I can't help it."

Mike patted the seat beside him, and I plopped down and began to relay what'd happened earlier at the soup kitchen and then the phone call. He listened and empathized. When I'd finished, he lifted my chin. "Look at me. You were worried about Isabella spending too much time with Tiffany with all her bad behavior. That woman just did all of us a favor. Now we won't have to put up with Tiffany anymore."

"I suppose. It doesn't feel good or right, though," I said as I thought about Tiffany having no friends. "Can you imagine the nerve of that woman calling Isabella a *ward*? Who uses that term, anyway? What a *stupid* woman!"

"Rosie, let it go. Let's enjoy our time together. Come on, let's try out that wine I bought. I'll get it. It's supposed to be good."

Although I knew letting go of my anger was necessary, I struggled. I was beginning to understand what it was like to be in a position to defend your child's actions, especially if they've been misrepresented. Without any question, I knew trouble was ahead.

Mike returned with two glasses of wine, and we sat together on the floor before the fire as if we were camping out. Sweet Pea had gone next door with Isabella, so she was not there to jump on us. After a while, Mike laid back on the floor and pulled me beside him. He cupped me against him, and I sighed with pleasure as his face lowered onto mine. We kissed until I felt my angst fade away. We talked and laughed about the first time we'd made love and the pleasant surprise that we fit together so well. I knew we'd be able to ensure that hadn't changed later.

Time slipped by. We reluctantly rose to fix dinner. While Mike grilled the steaks, I put together a green salad and set the table. We'd eat in the dining room with the good china and sterling silverware. I reached for the crystal wine glasses, set them out, and uncorked the second bottle of wine we'd have with dinner.

As we were eating, Mike's cell phone rang, and when he looked at it, he smiled and said, "Brian."

"Go ahead, answer it," I urged. I listened to Mike's half of the conversation. Brian, Mike's business partner, seemed to be checking in to talk. When there came a lull in the conversation, I signaled for Mike to hand over his phone.

"Hey, Cowboy!" I said, using my nickname for him. "Do you want to join us for Christmas in Santa Fe?"

"That sounds great. My parents are taking a Winter Holiday cruise and wanted me to join them, but I can't take the time."

"We're happy to have you with us, and I know Isabella will be pleased. Just let us know your itinerary, and we'll pick you up in Albuquerque." I handed the phone back to Mike.

"Sounds good, bro. I'll check in with you tomorrow. Bye."

Mike looked at me and shook his head with a big smile. "You and Isabella. You two are having fun building your family, aren't you?"

I smiled. "You bet. Just look at what we've created! Then, of course, there's you."

Mike's eyes softened, and he pulled me from my chair onto his lap. "Yes, my queen, there's me... always me."

I felt his hardness and whispered, "C'mon. I'll clean up the dishes tomorrow."

"I like how you think, woman," he said as he followed me upstairs.

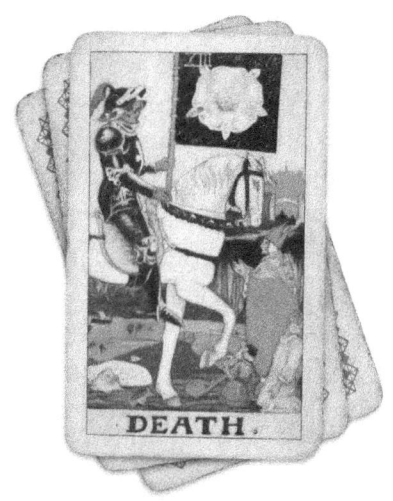

CHAPTER 26

L ate Monday morning, I received a telephone call from Isabella's school requesting that I meet with Dorothy Brookside and Alicia Johnson, the two headmistresses at The Wilson Charter School. I was pretty sure I knew what they wanted to discuss—Tiffany.

As I neared the school, I saw the same homeless woman, who had spoken to me the first time I'd been at the soup kitchen, bent over a homeless man. Next to her stood Red, our former site manager, tugging on the arm of the person on the ground. As I looked closer, it looked like it was Jerry, my fiancé's former police partner, lying on the ground. At first glance, it appeared he wasn't moving, and my heart dropped. Even though he'd tried to hurt me, I didn't want anything to happen to him because he was the only one who could tell us who murdered the two girls whose bones were at the construction site. After I passed,

I saw him stir in the rearview mirror. He was a mess, and I felt sorry for him. I wondered if he was homeless. And why was Red there? Were he and Jerry friends? Something to look into for sure, but for now, I drove on, not wanting to be late for my appointment.

The school was in session when I got there. When I entered the office area, I could hear the happy sounds emanating from the classrooms and muted tones of music coming from the music room down the long hallway. It was a pleasant place with good energy, and I was glad Isabella could attend school there. I announced myself to the receptionist and sat down to wait for the headmistresses. A short while later, Dorothy came to greet me.

"Hi Rosie, I'm glad to see you. Let's go into my office for some privacy, shall we?" I followed behind her as she looked over her shoulder and added, "Alicia will join us in a minute."

"Okay, that sounds good," I said.

"Ahh, here she is now," Dorothy announced as she entered her office.

"Hi, Rosie. Welcome to this wonderful madhouse!" said Alicia.

I smiled and sat in the seat they indicated at the table. "I love the sound of the kids busy at whatever they're doing—it provides beautiful music."

"Yes, I think so, too," said Dorothy. "Well, let's get to it, shall we? I understand that there was a problem at the soup kitchen on Saturday. Is that right?

"Unfortunately, that's true. I believe the mother of the girl involved would contact you regarding it. Did she?"

"Yes, she did, and both Alicia and I are very concerned about what happened. We also received a telephone call from Tiffany's mother, who asked us to separate Tiffany and Isabella. She also said she'd told you she didn't want Tiffany to have anything to do with Isabella and you. Is that right?"

My face flushed. "Yes, that's correct."

"We'd like to hear your version of what happened at the soup kitchen and anything else you have to tell us regarding Tiffany's behavior," said Alicia.

So I told them everything. When I finished, Alicia nodded to Dorothy. "You just agreed with Deborah's mother's story. Tiffany's behavior at your house is similar to what another mother said happened when her daughter befriended Tiffany last year," confirmed Dorothy.

"I don't know how Tiffany will survive if her parents don't straighten things out now. That girl will end up with no friends," I said, genuinely sorry for her.

"Her relationship with Isabella was doing Tiffany some good. Believe it or not, Tiffany's behavior these past few months has improved," said Dorothy.

"Off the record, we have requested counseling for the entire family. But that isn't looking as if it's going to happen. Her mother refuses to take part in it. Hopefully, she'll allow our school counselor to work with Tiffany individually," stated Alicia.

"Let's discuss Isabella's situation," said Dorothy. "Isabella is now in a challenging position. She's lost the friendship of a powerful young girl who has begun to talk poorly about Isabella. We have noticed a few of the students have stepped back from Isabella, wanting nothing to do with her not being bullied by Tiffany."

"Of course," added Alicia, "that makes us very unhappy, and we will be working with several of those girls individually to address what's happening to correct the situation. We will not tolerate any bullying."

"Do you have thoughts on the situation, Rosie?" asked Dorothy.

"Mike and I have been unhappy that Isabella has spent as much time as she has with Tiffany because of her behavior. Yet, we understand that Isabella is working through what she considers her humane responsibility to treat Tiffany well since Tiffany needs a friend."

"Isabella has a big heart, that's for sure," said Dorothy. "But there is no doubt that things will be difficult for both girls until things get straightened around. Alicia and I are concerned and want to ensure Isabella is okay through it all."

"We'll watch her and report anything we think is amiss. We know you and Isabella are close, and we want to make sure that she remains open with you about what's going on here," added Alicia.

"Thank you so much for your concern and help. Although Isabella is beyond her years in many ways, that doesn't mean she can't get hurt. I want to ensure that she doesn't feel she's being punished for something she's been falsely accused of doing."

"The truth will come out; it always does," said Dorothy. "It takes time, is all."

"That is what I'm worried about. Time can damage and destroy a person's image and self-esteem," I shot back.

"We'll work as quickly as possible so that doesn't happen," said Alicia. "Are you going away for the holidays?"

"Yes, we'll be in Santa Fe. Why?" I asked.

"That's good. Then the girls won't have an opportunity to meet up with each other," said Alicia.

"Isabella's dearest friends in Santa Fe will help her through this mess," I said. "She's been through so much. I hate to have another thing thrown at her."

"It's not always easy being a parent. We hate to see our children suffer when they have done nothing wrong," said Dorothy. "We'll do our best to get things straightened out as quickly as possible."

I nodded my head. "Please."

Alicia reached into her pocket, pulled out a small pink quartz heart, and placed it in my hand. "Here's a reminder to keep the faith, my friend."

I smiled. "Thank you both for your concern and kindness."

We said our goodbyes, and I left the school with a heavy heart for what Isabella was enduring and anger toward a young lady who didn't seem to have regard for anyone but herself.

After the school bus dropped Isabella off, she stormed through the door and slammed her books on the kitchen table. "I hate her, Mama! I hate her!"

"Is this about Tiffany?" I asked as I gathered Isabella to me while tears formed and fell from her dark eyes that snapped with anger. "Why don't you tell me what happened?" I murmured.

"She's telling people I'm to blame for the trouble at the soup kitchen. She said that I told her to beat up Deborah. And that's not true, Mama! You know it isn't!"

"No, that isn't true. Do you think the others believe you'd do such a thing?"

Isabella stared at me awhile in thought. "No, but that doesn't mean they will cross Tiffany and argue with her. They're afraid of her and don't want to be bullied by her."

"The truth will come out; it always does. Meantime, why don't you try to ignore her?"

"That shouldn't be hard to do since everyone knows I'm not allowed to be near her. Tiffany made sure of that," Isabella sputtered.

"What does Deborah have to say about that?"

"She hasn't been back to school, and Dr. Alicia told me she wouldn't be back until the first of the year."

"Oh, I see. Well, we're leaving for Santa Fe in a few days, so maybe with the start of a new year, things will be different when you return to school. Are you going to be okay for the next few days?"

"Yeah, I guess so."

"Just think; you'll see your sister-friends in a few days. That'll help, won't it?"

"Yes, it will!" she exclaimed. "And you'll get to see Auntie Karen too. Grandmother told us that something good always happens during bad times, too. Is that true?"

"It most certainly is. Just look at us. All the bad that happened to you brought me to you and you to me," I said, squeezing Isabella tight.

Isabella was quiet and then held out her hand to Sweet Pea. "And your lousy time brought you, Sweet Pea, didn't it?"

"Yes, it sure did," I said as my eyes watered. My fiancé's death had been a high price to pay for a dog—even the best dog in the world.

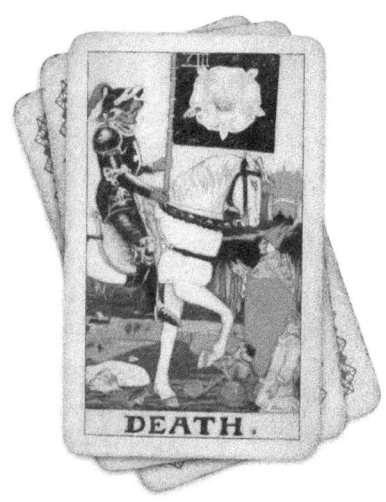

CHAPTER 27

❙❙ Hurry up, Isabella! The taxi is waiting," I called. Mike had already carried our bags to the driver to load into the car's trunk.

"Coming, Mama!" Isabella yelled as she pounded down the stairs with excitement. "I had to get my phone."

The plane was crowded, not unusual for the holiday season, and we pushed our way to a row of three empty seats. Sweet Pea was unhappy to be in her carrier, tucked beneath the seat before us. The flight was a short one, which made having her along manageable. I was looking forward to spending our holiday time in Santa Fe, which would be so different than all the past years for each of us. I knew Mike and Isabella were excited about it as well.

After we landed in Albuquerque, we went to get our rental car. Although we were renting a car for our time there, we'd agreed it made sense to purchase a vehicle in the spring and build a garage to house it after the frost was out of the ground.

As we waited for Mike to complete the paperwork, Isabella and I took Sweet Pea outside to go to the bathroom at the small dog park there. As we waited for her to do her thing, I spotted the same tall man I'd seen greet Johnny when I'd picked up Karen at the airport a few weeks ago. He stood beside a limo and bent over to speak to someone inside. He placed his right hand above the window to steady him, and I saw the same scorpion tattoo on the top of his hand as the two men who'd been murdered in Santa Fe wore. That meant he was connected to the Mexican group that'd taken over the border crossings and was cheating those wanting to cross over out of large sums of money. It also meant that he was most likely involved in the human trafficking ring that was taking place in New Mexico and beyond.

I saw Mike searching for us inside, and I waved to him. Once I got his attention, I signaled him to join us. "Quick, Mike. Look at the man leaning against the limo there. Can you make out the tattoo on his hand?" I whispered.

"What is it?" he asked in a soft voice.

"A scorpion. That's the group's name that's taken over the border crossings. He's the same man that picked up Johnny here at Thanksgiving time. Can you get a picture of him with your phone? Mine is at the bottom of my bag."

"Okay. Don't move, and I'll pretend I'm taking a picture of all of you."

A few minutes later, the limo's back door opened, and the tall man entered. The car took off, and we went to find our rental.

We drove into our driveway an hour later, and Isabella called, "Mama? Is that another dead crow on our door?"

My heart fell because it looked as if Isabella was right. When I'd first brought Isabella to Santa Fe and rented this house, there had been dead crows draped over the front door handle to scare me off. A ploy so I could leave Isabella in Santa Fe and run back to Las Vegas. Isabella's uncle Miguel had paid Coyote's nephew to put them there. Miguel's poor behavior had given way for Maria and me to be able to decide Isabella's fate to share the responsibility of raising her together.

"Not again," grumbled Mike. "That must mean that Coyote's nephew is out of rehab and back to drinking again. I'll call Coyote and see what's going on."

Determined not to have the dead crow spoil our holidays, I said, "C'mon, Isabella. Let's unpack so we can begin to decorate for Christmas."

Mike took pictures of the dead crow and cleaned up the mess. When he'd finished, he came inside. "I feel sorry for Coyote. He admitted that his nephew, Redmond, is back to drinking. His nephew probably doesn't realize that Miguel is not interested in paying him to do what he'd done in the past."

The doorbell rang, and the FedEx packages I'd shipped there arrived. Isabella opened the biggest box, which held the decorations. "Oh, how cute!" she squealed as she pulled out each item. Mike and I smiled at each other, enjoying her excitement. Then, Isabella and I began to set out the decorations around the house. At the same time, Mike opened and put together the fancy, fake Christmas tree that looked real enough that it'd be hard to tell the difference. The only thing missing was the smell of pine, but I'd bought pine-scented candles that would take care of that. Maria, Miguel, and their kids were coming to help decorate the tree the following night, and I'd invited Nica to join us, along with her Mother, Grandmother, and Coyote.

Our guests would arrive tomorrow afternoon—Karen and Brian from Boston, staying at the house with us, and Cal and Virginia from Las Vegas, staying at the Eldorado Hotel & Spa.

That night, after Isabella was settled in bed, reading her book, I handed Mike a nightcap of Amoretto and soda and joined him before the fire. "I'm concerned that trouble lays ahead."

"What do you mean?" asked Mike.

"Well, we have the dead crow back on the door, and when I was sitting with Grandmother over Thanksgiving break, I saw Maria's neighbor outside the café, hanging around. Grandmother warned me that more trouble was to come. I didn't want to think about it then, especially after all that happened, but Grandmother was right. I can feel it."

Mike looked thoughtful. "Well, let's keep this between us so we don't ruin the holidays for everyone. But at the same time, let's make sure the girls are safe. We'll have to keep an extra eye on them."

"I think I should remind Isabella to be careful, though. Especially since she's the oldest." "Probably not a bad idea," agreed Mike.

I rose from my chair.

"Where are you going?" asked Mike.

"I'll be right back."

When I entered Isabella's room, she looked up from her book with a smile. "Have you come to tuck me in?" That meant I'd join her for a few minutes to recap our day and discuss anything else.

"Yes, I have. It's been a pretty exciting day, hasn't it?"

"This is going to be the best Christmas yet!"

"I think so too. I want to make sure you girls stick together and are always aware of where you are. Tomorrow, there will be a lot of people around. I want to keep you safe."

Isabella studied me for a moment. "Do you feel it too, Mama?"

"Feel what?"

"There's trouble ahead for us, isn't there?"

"What do you mean?" I'd always known Isabella had psychic abilities, but I didn't realize how developed they were. I asked to see if what she said matched my worries.

"Mama, I had a vision where I saw everybody running around, looking for someone. Then you were crying. You said, 'Please, God, don't let anything happen to her.' Then I woke up."

I leaned forward and hugged her. "Yes, I'm certain there's trouble ahead. I don't know how it's all going to play out. You know, don't you, that you are like me? You can see into the future."

"And into the past, too, Mama."

I smiled. "Yes, there is that as well."

"So what do we do?" asked Isabella, worry on her brow.

"It never does any good to worry about things. We need to become the observer and observe everything around us—how people are acting and what they're saying. When something isn't right, we'll feel it in our gut," I said as I patted my belly.

Isabella nodded.

"Let's work together as a team, okay? We'll check in with each other, and if we feel something is off, we'll talk about it without bringing anyone else into our conversation."

"What about Mike?" Isabella asked.

"You can talk to him, too. You'll learn that not everyone is happy to be warned about an event that may occur in the future, especially if there's nothing they can do about it."

"That's for sure," said Isabella.

"Do you want to talk about it?" I asked.

She shook her head. "I like that we're going to be a team."

"Me, too. I don't want you to worry about anything. Just act normal, and we'll work it out together."

"Okay, Mama."

"Goodnight, Little One," I said as I stood and bent over to kiss her. Sweet Pea stirred beside Isabella and lifted her head for her kiss upon hearing the word goodnight. Isabella and I looked at each other and smiled.

I left with peace knowing my child and dog were tucked together in a warm, safe place. I returned to the front where Mike sat.

"Is everything okay?" he asked.

"Our Isabella has had a psychic vision of trouble ahead. I told her we'd work together to work it out, and she could also talk to you."

He nodded, and then a smile flashed. "Golly, between the two of you, do I stand a chance of surprising you with your Christmas gifts?"

I laughed as he pulled me into his lap. "Probably not."

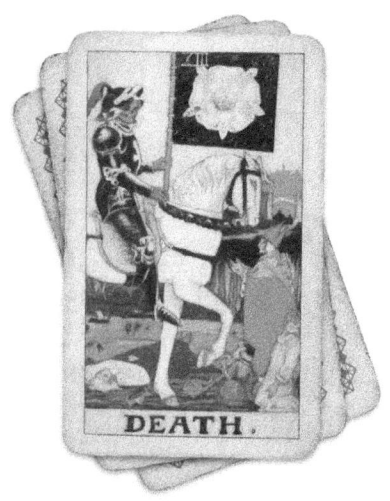

CHAPTER 28

T he next afternoon, large individual snowflakes with ornate designs began to float down from the heavens, announcing a white Christmas ahead. Mesmerized, Mike and I stood by the window and watched the snowfall. Soon, two cars pulled into the driveway, and car doors opened and slammed shut as people climbed out of the vehicles. Greetings were hollered back and forth as we opened the front door to Brian, Karen, Cal, and Virginia. Instead of having to drive to Albuquerque to pick them up, Brian and Cal rented a car there and drove here, saving us the trip.

"Merry Christmas, everyone!" shouted Isabella as she skirted around me to be the first to reach Grandfather, who looked enormously pleased with her doing so.

"Brrr. It's cold outside. Come on in and get warmed up," I said as I opened the door wider and stepped aside.

"I'll get the bags," offered Brian as he signaled Karen to go inside.

I hugged her as she passed me, and then I hugged Virginia, and finally, Cal, who continued holding Isabella against him.

"What a wonderful house!" Virginia exclaimed. "It's much bigger than it looks from the road." Everyone said that because the back end of the house didn't show from the front.

"How about a hot toddy for everyone?" Mike asked.

Brian stumbled through the doorway with two oversized suitcases and a carry-on. "Where do you want these, Karen?" he asked.

"Are all these yours?" I asked her.

Her cheeks flushed. "I'm afraid so." At my questioning expression, she added, "We'll talk later."

"I'll show you where they go, Uncle Brian. Follow me," said Isabella.

"Let's sit down and relax before the others join us," I suggested.

We sat with our steaming cups of punch on the extra stackable chairs we'd bought and placed strategically around the living room to accommodate all who would be here for the Christmas tree trimming party.

Shortly after we settled in, Coyote and Nica arrived. Isabella raced to the front door to let them in, and we heard squeals as the girls greeted each other. Then, Coyote stepped into the living, his eyes seeking out Karen. As soon as he spotted her, he beamed. "Merry Christmas, everyone," he said before heading to Karen and kissing her. We watched as they whispered between themselves, and then he took Karen's hand, pulling her from her seat. "Excuse us for a moment."

Karen led Coyote into Isabella's bedroom, where she'd be staying, and shut the door. Isabella and Nica watched them and then looked at each other and smiled. Isabella took Nica's hand and pulled her forward so she could introduce her to Cal, Virginia, and Brian.

Karen and Coyote emerged from the bedroom, Karen with pink cheeks and Coyote wearing a pleased expression. Something was up between them, and I wondered what it meant.

Noises and the sound of little voices drifted in from outside. Maria and Miguel, and their tribe had arrived. Isabella and Nica raced to the door and greeted them with "Merry Christmas" in one voice. They grabbed Angela and pulled her along so she could be introduced to Cal, Virginia, and Brian first.

Later, as I stood in the kitchen and listened to several conversations, mixed with the children's little voices raised in excitement, I looked to where Mike stood in the living room, smiling and ensuring everyone had what they wanted to drink. How I loved him and how I loved my new family!

I turned to watch Isabella play the hostess by pouring warm cocoa into the unique Christmas travel mugs she had chosen for the boys to use for this occasion. My eyes blurred with love, and my heart filled with gratitude for the opportunity to spend another lifetime with her. Sweet Pea was at her feet, and my spirit lifted upon seeing them together.

"Here," I said to Maria. "Let me take her."

I held my arms out to hold my namesake, Rosa, who'd soon be crawling and getting into all sorts of trouble. I jostled her up and down, making her laugh. I laughed, too, and looked to see Mike watching us with a smile. I took

Rosa's hand and waved to Mike. Then, I put her little hand on her mouth and opened it wide, blowing him a kiss. Rosa laughed and held her hand out for me to do it again.

Maria stepped to my side and squeezed my shoulder. "Merry Christmas, dear Rosie."

I wrapped my other arm around her shoulders and held her tight. "You are such a gift to me, my dear Maria. I'm so glad we're sister-friends."

"Hey, Mama and Aunt Maria, when are we going to decorate the tree?" asked Isabella as she came running up to me, breathless in her excitement.

"Here, Maria, take the baby. I've got to get the decorations, and then we can begin."

I carried out the big box of decorations with several smaller boxes on top. "Mike, why don't you turn on the tree lights so we can see where to place the Christmas decorations?"

When Mike plugged in the tree, and the lights flashed on, everyone raised their voice in appreciation, oohing, and aahing. The tree was spectacular, and no one seemed to mind that it wasn't real. "I have a special decoration for each of you to place on the tree. Miguel, will you help the little boys with theirs?"

The anger management course he was required to take as part of his atonement for paying to have dead crows placed at my house seemed to have helped. Instead of his usual scowl, he smiled and said, "Sure." Now that he wasn't so angry at everything, he had a twinkle in his eye and was quite handsome. It was the first time I could understand why Maria had been attracted to him in the first place.

I'd ordered different handmade decorations made from hand-blown glass with each one's name written on it. The little boys' decorations were of animals—a reindeer, a bear, and a dog. I was surprised at how excited they were as he placed their ball on the tree with reverence. After hanging our decorations on the tree, we admired it. Tears came to my eyes to see how many decorations signified a new family member. I felt blessed, and I knew Isabella felt the same way when she came to stand beside me. I squeezed her hand, and she tightened her grip on mine.

"Okay, here are the other decorations to add. Why don't you kids point to where you want us to place them, okay?"

*****

After everyone left except for us staying in the house, I spoke with Karen alone. "So what's going on, Karen?"

"Well, everything happened so fast that I didn't have a chance to do much more than pack and get here."

"What do you mean?"

"As you know, I've been toying with the idea of moving here with the possibility of teaching."

I nodded. "Yes."

"After I left here at Thanksgiving time, I put in a query to see what, if anything, was available at the Indian School at the Tesuque Pueblo. Surprisingly, they seemed interested in me and asked to see my resume. They interviewed me twice via Skype the following week and then sent me an offer last week. I accepted it as a first-grade teacher taking over for a teacher going on maternity leave beginning January 2nd."

"Wow, that's exciting. Then, you must have settled things with your boyfriend."

"Yes, ex-boyfriend now. I've got so much to do now. I have to find a place to rent and …."

"Whoa! Don't be silly," I interrupted. "Don't rush into finding a place. Stay here as long as you want. You can take over the guest room since we won't use it. Besides, that way, I know the house will be in good hands when we're not here."

Karen looked relieved. "Well, let me pay for the utilities, then."

"Deal," I said. "So, what's up with you and Coyote?"

Karen's pink cheeks reddened. "He wants to grow our relationship. He's called me every day since I left, and we've talked and talked. He says we belong together and told me Grandmother thinks so, too. I like what I see and what he has to say, and I didn't want to pass up the opportunity to see where our relationship takes us. I feel good about it, but I promise I won't rush into anything."

I almost laughed out loud because I believed she'd have to retract those words about not rushing into anything. It was easy to picture them together in the future, and I saw that things would happen quicker than she thought. But I was going to let her find that out for herself.

CHAPTER 29

I hadn't been able to sleep, so I'd crept out of bed, leaving Mike to sleep, and I made my way into the kitchen. Christmas Eve day had arrived with a six-inch cover of white snow, which made the outside look like a Christmas card. In my mind, there is an extraordinary beauty to any fresh snowfall that blankets the earth with its unique quietness. It's as if Mother Earth holds her breath for a few moments to enjoy what she's created.

I made a pot of coffee, poured myself a cup, and sat at the bar. I was surprised to see Brian wander in, and I got up to pour him a cup of coffee. I handed it to him with a smile. "Good morning, Cowboy. It sure is great to see you. We've missed you."

He kissed me on the cheek. "It's good to see you, too."

"So, how are things back in Boston?"

"Pretty good. The new guy is working out great, so I can join Mike in Las Vegas in a few weeks to help him with the new contract there. Working together on it shouldn't take us too long to get it done." He swallowed some coffee, then asked, "How's the construction going?"

"Something about the whole thing bothers me. We're losing our site foreman to Tony, who will build another gentlemen's club near us. Tony and Johnny will be working together. I don't know if Mike told you, but Johnny was meeting up with some other men in Santa Fe over Thanksgiving time. I think he and Tony will be involved in more human trafficking. Any thoughts?"

"I wouldn't be surprised if that were true. Interestingly, the two escaped all that happened at the Purple Passion Lounge. Their luck has to run out sometime—maybe sooner than later. What about that Jerry guy? Is he still out, waiting for a hearing?"

"He's a hot mess. I saw him passed out on the street. When I drove by that way again, he was gone. I've even tried calling his cell phone, and there's no service. Frankly, I think he's homeless. And that's not good because I don't want anything to happen to him, especially since I think he knows who committed the killings."

Mike entered the kitchen and poured himself a cup of coffee. He came to where I sat and kissed me. "Good morning, my queen," he murmured into my ear. He turned to Brian, "What are you two up to?"

"Rosie's catching me up on the latest with Johnny and Tony."

"Ah, yes. Those two. Amazingly, they've been able to keep out of trouble with the police. It doesn't seem right, especially when we know they were involved with everything happening at the Purple Passion Lounge."

"I was telling Brian that they will continue to be involved in human trafficking. Oh, and I haven't had the chance to tell him about the man we saw who had the scorpion tattoo."

"Scorpion tattoo?" asked Karen as she joined us in the kitchen. "Isn't that the group that Coyote was telling us about that rules the border crossings?"

"The very same one," I said as I rose to make another pot of coffee.

Karen took my place at the counter. "Coyote says that he believes those are the people responsible for the deaths of the two men murdered here. He just can't prove it."

"That's the problem with so many unresolved cases. It takes time to build up a case," Brian said.

We nodded in agreement. Then Karen asked, "What's the plan today, Rosie?"

"Everyone is free to do what they want until five o'clock. Then it'll be just Cal and Virginia joining us here for a simple supper of baked ham, potato casserole, and green beans with dessert. At 2 o'clock, Mike, Isabella, and I are going to Maria's house to exchange our gifts."

"Oh," said Karen. At the look on her face, I added, "You're going to be spending Christmas Eve with Coyote, aren't you?"

"Yes, if you don't mind. I'll be sleeping here, though."

I smiled. "Sounds good, then."

"Brian and I have some errands to run, but I'll be back to help you before we go to Miguel's. You said you need me to pick up a few things?" asked Mike.

I nodded. "I have a list made, ready for you."

"For now, who wants breakfast?" Mike asked.

"I do," said a young voice as Isabella joined us, Sweet Pea at her heels.

I opened my arms wide, and she came to me. "What time do we go to Angela's?" she asked. I smiled because Mike, Isabella, and I had named the place we were going to after the person most important to us.

"Two o'clock. If you need to do any shopping, I can take you after I fix the casserole and get dressed."

"I'll help you, and Isabella and I can set the table. Before Coyote picks me up, I'd like to tag along with you to do a little shopping, if you don't mind."

When it was time to leave, I went into my bedroom to grab my purse. In doing so, I knocked it over, spilling out some of the contents. I'd had every intention of removing my tarot cards before we came for the holidays, but it was now obvious I hadn't done so. There they were, spilled across the dresser with the Death card on top. I groaned. Why hadn't I remembered? "I know, I know," I whispered. "Things happen for a reason." Pushing worry aside, I went to join Isabella and Karen.

CHAPTER 30

A t two o'clock, Mike, Isabella, and I loaded several bags of presents into our car and headed to Maria's house. We could hear the boys and their noisy play from the outside, and we smiled at each other and readied ourselves before I rang the bell. With a clump of loose hair that'd fallen from her ponytail, Maria answered the door and looked frazzled. But she smiled and laughingly said, "You'll never guess what Santa left as an early Christmas present."

A black nose peeked out from between her legs, and the cutest golden retriever puppy yipped at us, protesting our disturbing her fun. The three boys scrambled to move her out of the way. Then Miguel called them to come away from the door so we could enter. It was a madhouse!

Isabella raced to Angela, who sat on the floor next to the tree, trying to keep Rosa from pulling down the

169

decorations within her reach. Rosa's stretchable playpen area was used to keep the yapping puppy inside, and Maria was frantically searching for the baby walker to put Rosa in. I looked at Mike and laughed. The others heard me and looked at me in surprise. Then, they began to join in my laughter too.

After Rosa was placed in her walker and the puppy settled, Maria welcomed us warmly. Miguel stepped forward, shook Mike's hand, and greeted me with a Merry Christmas. We sat in the living room with eggnog, and when it was time, Mike handed out the presents one by one. Maria and I had agreed that we'd buy only one present for each person or we could double up if needed. I'd gotten Maria's permission for my chosen gifts, so there wouldn't be any issues.

Success! Each child exclaimed over the present that we presented to them. All seemed satisfied with what we'd chosen for them, as did Maria and Miguel.

We had given Armando and Ricardo (the older boys) an Xbox player and little Miguel a computer game that taught him math, reading, and puzzles. The boys became so intrigued with the gifts that they missed seeing Rosa's face light up with the distinctive music box that would supposedly be a collector's item in the future. It could be played before bedtime or anytime, with long-playing musical choices, and Rosa instinctively swayed to the rhythm of the song playing.

Isabella waited patiently for her turn to present Angela with a round-trip plane ticket to Las Vegas inside a travel suitcase she'd picked out. Angela would visit for a few days during spring break. "You're going to love it!" predicted Isabella as she pushed the large box forward.

Angela opened the box, saw her suitcase, and then the envelope with the airline ticket inside. Angela's eyes got big, and she squealed, "I do! I do love it!"

Maria laughed when she opened the Christmas card I'd handed her with a gift certificate for a spa weekend at the nearby Eldorado Hotel & Spa. "Heavenly! A special time for you and me, Miguel—alone."

He nodded, pleased.

Angela rose and held her hand out for Isabella to take. "Come see what we got you!" she said as she led Isabella into the bedroom they'd be sharing. Waiting with a big bow on each item was a brand new twin bed and matching bureau, just like Angela's. Isabella's face lit up, and she ran and jumped on her bed, laughing. "Thank you so much!"

I handed Mike the Christmas card Maria had passed us to open. I was thrilled to see it was a gift certificate for dinner and our pick of a show at the International Shakespeare Center in Santa Fe. I wasn't sure what Mike thought about it, although he smiled pleasantly and thanked everyone.

I helped Maria pick up all the wrappings and empty boxes. Then, it was time for us to return to the house in time to greet Cal and Virginia. Before we left, Brian said that he was going to take a nap. Hopefully, he'd been able to sleep because he'd looked exhausted with dark circles under his eyes when he arrived. After all the excitement of being at Maria's house, I looked forward to a calmer evening with our family.

When we got home, I was delighted to see that Brian had turned on the Christmas tree lights, which showed through the window, welcoming us. As we drove further in the driveway, it felt almost eerie that the house belonged to me because it signified all the changes in my life for it to have become mine. So much had happened! I whispered my thanks to the Universe. Then I exited the car in time to greet Cal and Virginia, who drove in behind us. Cal carried a large manila envelope in one hand while his other arm circled Virginia in a cuddling fashion.

I was tired and relieved that dinner was prepared. All I had to do was pop the potato casserole into the oven, heat the string beans with almonds, and put out the Honey-Baked ham. We each would serve ourselves when it was time to eat. I set out snacks and then settled in before the fire. Cal and Virginia sat on the couch with Isabella between them. They hovered over the paperwork that Isabella held in her lap, showing different furniture choices, bedspreads, and lamps she could choose from for her room in Cal's new house. They were laughing, asking each other what their favorites were when I felt a chill and goosebumps raced across my body. At the same time, Isabella must have felt it, too, for she looked at me with a questioning expression. I held my hands out and shrugged my shoulders. She looked worried but went back to what she'd been doing. It happened so quickly that no one else seemed to notice our exchange. Something was up, for sure. We'd been forewarned.

When the Death card reared its ugly head, I always became anxious; this time was no exception. My cell phone rang, and I jumped. When I saw it was Mimi, I answered with a cheery, "Merry Christmas, girlfriend!"

"I just wanted to wish you all a Merry Christmas tonight since tomorrow I know you'll have everyone there for dinner."

"How are things with you?" I asked. "How's your dad?"

"He's doing okay for being so sick. But I think he will be around for some time to come."

I took a deep breath, glad for her and relieved that the Death card wasn't for her. "Here, let me put you on speaker so everyone can say hello."

We all had something to say, even Isabella, who stood by me. After we'd finished the call, she asked, "Do you think we should call Romano and Uncle Randy?"

I felt they were okay, so I said, "No, they're with friends, and they said they'd call tomorrow." I squeezed her against me and whispered, "We'll just have to wait and see what happens."

CHAPTER 31

Virginia and I were cleaning up the dirty dishes and straightening the kitchen before we joined the guys for an after-dinner drink when we heard a car pull into the driveway. It must be Coyote and Karen returning, and I wondered why she was back so early.

I went to the front door to let them in, and when I opened it, I was shocked to see Karen in disarray and Coyote's condition not much better. Karen's mascara was smeared, and her eyes were red from crying. "What's wrong?" I asked, panicked. "Come inside."

They walked in together as if in a daze. "It's Redmond," Coyote finally said. "We found him dead... an overdose. Seeing him like that has been tough on Karen," he said, holding her close. "I think a good stiff drink is what she needs right now. Sorry, I can't stay. I have to see to things."

"I understand," I said. "C'mon with me, Karen."

Before releasing her, Coyote pulled Karen toward him, giving her a long, passionate kiss. "I'll see you tomorrow, sweetheart."

Karen nodded numbly. I wrapped my arms around her, hugging and kissing her wet cheek before she let me lead her into the living room while Coyote turned and left. It was a sad time as we sat and listened to Karen's story of how she and Coyote had found Redmond. He hadn't shown up the night before, which wasn't unusual for him. But when he was still missing for their holiday meal, they had gone to look for him and had found him in an empty barn on the reservation, not far from the house.

A short while later, Karen excused herself and headed for bed. "Goodnight, all. Please don't let what happened take away the joy of you all being together here. I know how much this means to Rosie and Isabella."

Holidays were challenging for many of us because it was a time of awareness of who was no longer with us. With a heavy heart, I watched Karen leave. Isabella gave me a look that meant she wanted to talk.

"Isabella, why don't we get your stocking to hang up on the mantle?"

She nodded and followed me into my bedroom. "Mama, is that why we felt something was wrong?"

"I believe so, but I'm not sure."

"Me, either."

When we returned to the living room, I looked at Brian, who sat away from everyone, studying the flames dancing in the fireplace. Then I remembered that he had lost his sister to suicide around the holidays a few years ago. I knew I needed to do something to liven things up, so I began to sing "White Christmas." Slowly, the others started to join in. We went on to sing other favorites, and our spirits lifted, especially with recognizing our responsibility that life was for the living. I looked at Isabella, whose face glowed with happiness, and I knew how important this time was for her—her first Christmas as my daughter. I blew her a kiss and kept on singing.

After a while, Cal and Virginia rose to take their leave. They'd return the next day at 10 o'clock to celebrate Christmas with us. Then, Isabella said goodnight to Mike and Brian and headed into her bathroom to get ready for bed without disturbing Karen, who was asleep.

I took Sweet Pea back to the patch of stones that Mike had cleared for her to use for her daily duties. I waited for her to finish and then took her inside to tuck her in beside Isabella.

"Merry Christmas. I love you, Little One," I said.

"I love you always and forever, Mama." There it was again. That special pledge of love that I found so endearing.

"Ditto," I said as I kissed her head.

CHAPTER 32

T he following day was a mixture of fun, laughter, and sporadic moments of grief, remembering Redmond's sad passing. But, overall, everyone rallied, wanting to make this Christmas special for Isabella. We took turns opening presents and laughed at Brian as he strutted around with the new cowboy hat Mike and I had given him. He certainly was handsome, I thought. Some girl would be lucky to round him up.

"Cowboy, the only thing you need now is a horse," I teased.

"Maybe next year," he laughed.

It was fun to watch Isabella open her gifts one at a time—slowly and carefully. Cal had gifted her a trip to Disney World with the rest of us—a family trip. Isabella looked at me with glowing eyes. "I've never been to Florida. Have you, Mama?"

"No, I haven't been there either. It's going to be so cool for all of us to go there together, isn't it?"

She hesitated. "Yes, but …"

"But what?"

"What about Nica and Angela? They'll want to go, too."

"Would you like them to join us?" Cal asked.

Isabella studied him and nodded her head. "Yes, Grandfather."

"Then, we'll invite them, okay?"

Isabella raced to his chair and threw her arms around him. "Oh, thank you, Grandfather."

Cal looked at me and winked. He was getting such pleasure out of being the Grandfather, able to spoil Isabella, which was fine by me. Virginia sat next to him, looking pleased.

"We'll have to make it a summer visit, Cal."

He nodded.

Later, each of us moved our presents into our bedrooms, and Cal took his gifts and Virginia's out to their car. It was interesting to see that Mike and I had the same idea of a cuff bracelet as our Christmas gift to each other. I wasn't sure that Mike would be willing to wear it every day, but he immediately put his on with a big smile. His bracelet was very masculine, with a big turquoise stone centered and etchings around it. My bracelet was much daintier with a combination of turquoise and coral stones. I loved it!

I checked my watch to see that I had enough time before the others joined us for a Mexican Christmas spread to see Grandmother. Under the circumstances, she and her daughter wouldn't be coming for dinner. It was a relief to know that the preparations for dinner were under control. Besides Maria bringing her famous flan for dessert, all the other food would be prepared by my favorite restaurant and delivered to us. Mike and I thought that would be the easiest thing to do for everyone involved. He'd even joked, "After all, we're in New Mexico, so why not do what the natives do?" even though I knew not everyone served Mexican dishes for their Christmas dinner.

I went to find Mike to tell him what I wanted to do.

"Go, and don't worry. I'll hold down the fort until you get back. Is Karen going with you?"

"Yes, and Isabella too. We won't be long. I need to check on Grandmother and make sure she's okay."

"I understand," he said, pulling me into his arms and kissing me.

I packed some food and special holiday treats before we loaded into the rental car and headed out. The roads were cleared of snow and were in good shape to drive. Karen sat, worried. She'd spoken to Coyote, and he was waiting for her to arrive. Coyote was standing by the fountain in the center of the small village when we got there. Immediately he came to us. He pulled Karen to him and held on as if never to let her go. He was a wreck. I knew he felt he hadn't done enough to save Redmond while, at the same time, he was smart enough to know you can't save anybody … you can only save yourself.

I grabbed the food basket and bag of presents and took hold of Isabella's hand to head to Grandmother's house, leaving Karen and Coyote behind. When we arrived, Grandmother was standing in the open doorway, waiting for us, which was no surprise with her psychic abilities. "Come, my daughters," she said, holding her hand out in greeting. As we stepped forward, she kissed each of us before we stepped inside.

After she shut the door, I turned back to her. "How are you, Grandmother—my mother?"

"At peace, knowing Redmond is in a safe place. Nica's mother hasn't reached that point yet, but she has been through this before when her husband died. She needs some time."

"What can I do?"

"Take Nica back with you so the child knows some joy celebrating the Great Spirit on this day."

"Would it help her to stay with us for a few days?"

"I think so. Let's check with Nica's mother."

My heart went to Nica's beautiful mother, ravaged by grief. I bent and kissed her, saying, "I'm so sorry."

Grandmother spoke to her in Tewa, which I couldn't understand. Then Nica's mother lifted her face, smiled, and nodded. "Thank you, Rosie. It'd be best to have Nica away from here for a bit."

Isabella helped Nica pack a few things while I sat with Grandmother in the kitchen. "Grandmother, you said there was more trouble to come?"

She patted my hand and was quiet. Finally, she nodded, "Not here, though."

I felt goosebumps crawl along my body. Grandmother's message was loud and clear. Not here meant that trouble awaited us in Las Vegas, and I knew with certainty that she was right. But what could it be?

"Ready, Mama?" called Isabella as she and Nica bypassed the kitchen and headed to the front door to wait for me.

I rose from the table and kissed Grandmother on both wrinkled, weathered cheeks. When I searched her eyes, she patted my hand. "I love you, my daughter. Keep Isabella safe."

My heart dropped. Was Isabella not safe? She'd been through so much already. I'd do my best to protect her. I only hoped I could.

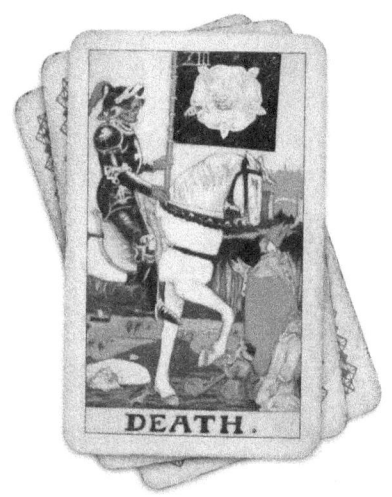

CHAPTER 33

T he next few days were hectic. Cal and Virginia left the day after Christmas, returning to Las Vegas. They weren't used to all the confusion, and I couldn't blame them for wanting to escape. Besides, they had a lot to do to prepare for their move into their new digs. Virginia and I had never reached Cal's house to help him sort through some of his mother's things, so we rescheduled that for the first of the year. Cal had plenty of time and was in no rush to move until he had everything in place. Virginia needed to leave her rental home by the end of January.

To our disappointment, Brian also left the day after Christmas, flying back to Boston. He'd promised his new employee extra time off during the holidays to spend with his family, which meant that Brian would cover the office. Mike didn't say much, but I knew it wasn't easy for him to sit still because he was anxious to return to Las Vegas and work.

Redmond's death had taken its toll on everyone. It wasn't that the holidays were utterly ruined, but the extra joy was gone. Even the girls were subdued. However, the idea of them going together to Disney World during the summer gave them something to look forward to, and they constantly talked about it as if to get past what'd happened recently with the death of Redmond. I was particularly concerned about the effect on Nica, but she seemed to rally around the other two girls.

Karen spent the majority of her time with Coyote when he was available. He was struggling with what'd happened to Redmond. With Karen's calm demeanor and down-to-earth sense about her, he was learning to let go of some of his guilt and better able to get on with his life. Coyote wasn't convinced that Redmond had died by his own hand. The rest of us remained quiet, not challenging his opinion but letting him work things out.

However, I had enough time with Karen to help her get settled in the guest room for her time there. We sat together and reviewed the list left with me when I bought the house, showing the different vendors for the services needed to maintain it. Now that Brian was gone and Karen had taken over the guest room, Angela came to join Isabella and Nica for two nights of sleepovers. Then, Maria asked all three girls to go to their house.

I drove the girls to Maria's house and returned by myself, feeling as if I'd forgotten something—that feeling that comes after someone leaves your life, if only for a few hours. It was amazing how attached I was becoming to Isabella.

When I got home, I began straightening up the house and putting away some Christmas items.

Mike came through the door, paused, and said, "Where is everybody? It sure is quiet."

"Ah, my good man. It seems we have the house to ourselves until Karen returns for the night."

"So, my queen, can you guess what time it is?"

"I might," I smiled. "Just what is it you have in mind?"

"Come with me, and I'll show you," he said as he lifted me into his arms and carried me into the bedroom.

CHAPTER 34

A fter dinner, we sat before the fire with an after-dinner drink and talked about what we needed to do in Santa Fe before leaving in two days and returning to Las Vegas. Mike agreed to speak to the contractor doing the construction work at Maria's and Miguel's house to get an estimate for the work we wanted done to build a garage. The following day, we'd begin to look at used cars since Karen would be staying at the house and would need a car to use until hers arrived in a few weeks from Boston. If we didn't find a car, I'm sure that Coyote would offer her to stay with him at the Pueblo if necessary.

We heard a truck pull in, and soon both Karen and Coyote came through the door. "Hi, there, you two. Join us? How about a nightcap?" I asked as I rose from my chair and went into the kitchen. I returned with two drinks and handed them each one.

"How are things going for you, Coyote?" asked Mike. "It's been a tough time for you."

"Yes, it sure has. Thank God for Karen being here and helping me through this," he said as he looked at Karen with love and pulled her close. He frowned. "I don't believe that Redmond was alone when he died. Something isn't sitting right with me."

"What does Grandmother think?" I asked.

"She refuses to answer me. Says that I'll work it out. What the hell does that mean? Work it out?" he asked, annoyed.

"What do you think, Rosie?" asked Karen.

"I don't know." Karen seemed surprised at my answer, so I quickly added, "I have so much on my mind that I haven't stayed quiet long enough to get any messages. I'll let you know if and when I do, though."

"Let's face it. There's no easy answer staring us in the face. Maybe Grandmother is right, though, and it'll work itself out in time," Coyote said begrudgingly.

"I agree," said Karen. "Time will tell."

"Coyote, did Mike tell you about the man we saw at the airport? The same man that had greeted Johnny at Thanksgiving time?"

"Yes, I have the sheriff in Albuquerque working on that because we know that some members of the Scorpion gang are here illegally to get revenge on those who opted out. What a mess that's been since the Scorpions believe those people took money from them, which I find hard to believe from the two murders we looked into here. Those guys didn't seem to have much money at all. I don't know why they bothered to kill them; it doesn't make sense."

A strange feeling came over me. "Maybe it's not about the money but their knowledge of how the gang deals with human trafficking."

"Do you mean those murdered might have been involved in blackmailing them?" asked Mike.

I nodded.

"Hmm. That makes sense. We'll have to look more into that angle," Coyote said.

"We also learned something else, Coyote," I said. "Johnny Cardoza is getting back together with his old boss, Tony, whom he was involved with the auctioning off the girls at the Purple Passion Lounge in Las Vegas. Tony is building a new Gentlemen's club there, which means they'll probably return to their old tricks."

"Wow, that's interesting." With a frown, Coyote added, "How are they getting away with that?"

"Good question," said Mike.

Karen looked exhausted when she and Coyote first came inside, and I smiled when I saw her on the couch, slumped against Coyote with his arm nestled around her. They fit together like some couples who look like they belong together. There was no question in my mind that we'd have a wedding to attend—much sooner than Karen realized. I looked at Mike and smiled. I wondered if I could say the same for us. Was there going to be a wedding for us too?

Karen stirred, and Coyote tenderly shook her awake. "Time for bed, darling. Come on, and I'll tuck you in," he said as he led her into the guest room.

It wasn't too much later that we heard Coyote coming toward us. Mike and I looked at each other and didn't say a word. He looked as exhausted as Karen had. "Man, this has been a long day."

Mike rose from his chair and extended his hand. "Take care, Coyote. And call me if there's anything I can do to help you."

"Do you have time to look at Redmond's death scene tomorrow?" he asked. "I'd like to hear what you think about it."

"Sure. What time do you want to meet?"

"How about ten o'clock at my office?"

"Okay, I'll be there."

"Thanks. That means a lot." Coyote came to where I sat and bent to kiss me on the cheek. "Goodnight, Rosie."

I watched Mike walk Coyote to the front door, locking it afterward. Two handsome men, for sure.

"Well, I guess I know what Karen and I will be doing tomorrow," I said as Mike entered the living room.

"Car hunting?" asked Mike.

"Yup," I said. "The first look, anyway."

Mike pulled me up from my chair. "You've got a lot to do tomorrow, then. I know how fussy you can be about picking out fruit, so I can imagine how you'll be about picking out a car," he teased. "C'mon, woman, time for bed."

CHAPTER 35

I awoke and smiled. Sweet Pea's head was close to Mike's, her breathing in rhythm with his. Mike took up enough room so that for Sweet Pea to be able to stay on the bed without being kicked off, she had no choice but to become an appendage to Mike.

As soon as I stirred, two things happened simultaneously: Mike reached for me at the same time as Sweet Pea jumped over me to get away from Mike rolling onto her. They startled each other with their actions, which made me laugh out loud. Mike pulled me closer and teased, "Gotcha!" as he tickled me.

Sweet Pea went wild, barking, trying to get between us. We laughed at her antics, and I thought, what a delightful way to begin the day. Maybe today would be a good day for all of us—undoubtedly more cheery than the past few days.

The scent of fresh coffee brewing came wafting in. Knowing Karen was awake, I kissed Mike lovingly and climbed out of bed. "I love you, handsome," I said with a smile.

"Ah, my queen, I love you, too," he said in a husky voice.

Stepping into the kitchen, I noticed Karen looked more rested than I'd seen her in the past two days. "Did you have a good sleep?" I asked.

"I slept like a log for a change, thank God."

"Are you up for some car shopping?"

"Sure. Maybe that will distract me from seeing Redmond lying dead on the barn floor. It's like a bad dream that I can't seem to shake."

"Okay, let's see if we can find a cute set of wheels. Remember that time we looked for a car to buy for me at Cornell?"

Karen chuckled. "Who could forget? We only cared about whether the car was cute and not how it worked. We were going to buy that car we loved without test-driving it first. Then we thought better of it. Good thing we did a test drive because it turned out to be a piece of junk."

I laughed, "At least the salesperson had the grace to be embarrassed."

Karen smiled. "He tried to wiggle his way around it by asking us out for drinks, remember?"

"I do, indeed. He looked rather surprised it would include four of us," I laughed. "It's good that by now, we know better what to look for in a car."

She smiled. "I need a quick bite to eat and a shower, and I'll be ready to go."

"Me, too."

"Good morning, ladies," said Mike coming into the kitchen. "Anyone for scrambled eggs?"

"Yes," Karen and I chimed together, then looked at each other and smiled. I reached for a mug, poured Mike coffee, and handed it to him.

"Coyote said that the used car place down the road is a good place to start. He says the guys there are honest and can be trusted," said Mike.

"Good to know," I responded.

After breakfast, we headed out at the same time—Mike to meet Coyote and us girls to the car dealers down the road. Mike had left the rental car for us while he walked the few blocks to Coyote's office. I'd quickly called Isabella to tell her we'd pick her up later. It was to be our last night in Santa Fe, and it would be a quiet one before we headed home to Las Vegas the following night to celebrate New Year's there.

I felt relaxed for the first time in several days as Karen, and I took a cursory view of the cars on display. Two of them looked like a possibility. I had decided that I wanted an SUV because, with its additional space, we'd be able to haul things when needed. There was a Honda SUV and a Nissan SUV available. When we stopped for a closer look at the Honda, we heard the salesman behind us tell the story we all hear whenever we look at a car for sale—"Yep, we just got this beauty in. You're the first to see it..."

We took turns sitting in both cars, one right after the other and decided to test-drive them. The Nissan was bright orange, which had grown on me, although it would not blend in with the crowd on the road. Two hours later, I signed the preliminary papers for the Nissan. I'd sent Mike the particulars with photos over my cell phone, and he was adamant that we not delay buying it—especially since the salesman would get the car registered that afternoon. It was still under warranty, and we had five days to consider the car or refuse it—the lemon law. It would be easy for me to get insurance coverage over the telephone with the agent that Coyote recommended so that it would all be ready for Karen to drive it by the end of the day.

After signing the papers, I asked Mike if he and Coyote wanted to meet us for a late lunch in town. They agreed, and we went to my favorite restaurant for Mexican food. Karen and I looked up as they walked in the door—each tall, dark, and handsome. My heart lifted when I saw them, and I knew Karen felt the same by the blush on her cheeks.

As our meals were served, I asked Mike, "Did you check out the barn at the Pueblo?" He nodded, and I asked, "What did you think? Any new perspective on it?"

He looked around, saw that the restaurant was crowded, and hesitated to discuss it publicly. "We'll talk later. After lunch, Coyote and I have more work to do."

"Oh, I see."

Karen was eying Coyote, searching for answers. Coyote nodded perceptively, and we all remained quiet.

To change the subject, Coyote said, "Orange, huh? Your new car is orange?"

"A sedate color, it's not," I laughed. "But the car is great… even has heated seats, which has to be a must here in the winter."

Coyote laughed. "Yes, it helps. I even have them in my truck."

Karen and I ordered dessert, but Mike and Coyote were anxious to get out and finish up their work. Mike paid the bill, and then they were off. As we ate our flan, I asked Karen, "Have you talked to our other sister-friends yet?"

She shook her head and sighed. "I didn't want to worry them over the holidays, but I will call them the day after New Year's, okay?"

"Sure. Then let me know afterward so I can follow up with them. You have a lot to talk about, especially since you've accepted a new teaching job here in Santa Fe. I know they'll be surprised but happy for you, though, and I don't want to spoil your fun by telling them."

Karen's eyes twinkled. "Yes, quite a jump for me to make, wasn't it?"

"Indeed." I thought how brave she was to take the step she had, and yet, it felt right. My intuition told me that she'd made the right choice. I was happy to be there for her for the first few days of adjusting to the house. Tomorrow, we would leave late to arrive home amidst the confusion and celebration of New Year's Eve – probably not the best planning considering the mobs that would've come into the city to celebrate. But then, it was what it was.

CHAPTER 36

II It's okay, Sweet Pea. You're okay," I said to her in a soothing tone as we disembarked from the airport. She'd heard a few firecrackers go off before the big show scheduled for later that night and now was shaking and trying to escape her pet carry-on bag, making it difficult for Isabella to hold onto it.

"Don't be afraid, Sweet Pea. I'll protect you," promised Isabella as we loaded into our parked car to head home.

"Ah, home sweet home," said Mike with a shake of his head as he pulled the car into heavy traffic. "There's always something going on here in Las Vegas."

When we pulled into our driveway, I became uneasy and looked around to see what had caused that feeling. Something wasn't right.

"Mama, do you feel it?"

I turned to look at Isabella, leaning forward from the backseat.

"Yes, I do," I answered. "Mike, you'd better check the house before we go in. Something isn't right." He looked at me with concern. "Both Isabella and I feel something is off."

"Okay, ladies. You stay here, and I'll be right back. Lock the doors," he ordered.

It was a very long ten minutes before he returned. "Yup, you were right. Someone broke in while we were gone. It looks like all they wanted was food. I couldn't see that they had taken anything. We'd better call the police to check this out. Maybe you girls can go next door until we figure out what happened."

I groaned. "Oh, my. I hate to disturb Irene and Ron, but we have no choice. Come on, Isabella, and bring Sweet Pea too."

I was so lucky to have my neighbors. After her grandchildren had moved away, Irene had become Gramma Irene to Isabella, and she now treated Isabella as if she were her granddaughter, making both of them happy.

Ron has taken part in the time my former boss blamed me for messing up her life and wanted to kill me after I abducted the little girls scheduled to be auctioned off in a sex trafficking scheme. Ron had been a hero that day and continued to act as one. I had to bite my tongue at times because of it, but fair was fair, he'd helped to save my life, and he deserved to be honored.

When Ron heard what happened, he immediately donned his jacket and raced to join Mike to "give him a hand."

Sitting in their living room, we saw the twirling lights of the two patrol cars, which pulled into the driveway without sirens. Amazingly, a few minutes after entering the house where Mike and Ron were waiting for them, the police came back out and left.

Sweet Pea barked at the knock on the door, and Irene got up to unlock it. Mike and Ron stood there.

"C'mon in, you two," she invited, waving them inside.

"What happened? The police weren't there that long," I asked.

"This is a busy night for them. Because there was no real damage and nothing was stolen, they told us to call tomorrow if we find anything was taken," Mike responded.

"Oh, that's understandable since it is New Year's Eve."

"C'mon, my ladies. Let's get home before the fireworks begin in earnest. Thanks, Ron and Irene, for helping out."

"Yes, thank you," I said. "And Happy New Year."

"And to you all," said Irene as Ron placed his arm around her and held her close. I smiled. They looked more like children in height than the adults they were.

Isabella kissed them both and left with Sweet Pea in her arms. I followed behind, staying close.

Mike grabbed our bags from the car and brought them inside. It didn't take long to unpack enough to set things aside to deal with the next day. Although we all were tired, only Isabella put on her jammies, ready for bed. As I lay beside her in bed for our usual bedtime chat, I asked a worried Isabella, "What's on your mind, Little One?"

"I don't like the feeling that someone has been in our house. Do you think it's someone we know?"

"I'm not certain, but it makes sense, doesn't it?"

She nodded. "It feels funny to be here in Las Vegas, and my friends are back in Santa Fe. I miss them already."

"I know what you mean. Karen is back in Santa Fe too. But it's up to us, Isabella, to stretch beyond what we're comfortable with to allow others into our life. It'd be wonderful if you brought one of your schoolmates home for dinner one night this week. Think about who you'd want to have, and I'll call her parents."

"Mama? Can I ask a boy for dinner instead of a girl?"

"I guess so. Do you have someone in mind?"

She smiled and nodded.

"I haven't heard you talk about him before. What's his name?"

"Sammy. You'll like him. He's one of us."

"What do you mean?"

"He sees into the future like we can."

"Really. How interesting."

"I know," she said with a smile.

"Well, ask him tomorrow, and I'll call his mother."

"Thanks, Mama."

"Goodnight, sweetheart, and Happy New Year," I said as I bent down and kissed her goodnight. I did the same to Sweet Pea, who was tucked in tight next to Isabella, innately knowing more fireworks were coming. I rose and headed to the door.

"Happy New Year, Mama. I love you forever."

"And I, you, Little One. Always."

When I joined Mike downstairs, he'd poured each of us a glass of champagne. "I know you're as tired as I am, so let's toast in the New Year now. Of course, I can think of a better way to celebrate."

"You can? Do you have something in mind?" I teased.

He set his drink down and gently removed the glass from my hand, placing it on the counter. He positioned his hands on each side of my head and lowered his mouth onto mine. His kiss was tender yet urgent. When he heard me moan, he pushed me further back against the counter, his body pressing against mine. "God, Rosie, you make me crazy with love for you. Screw the champagne; let's go upstairs now."

I smiled. "I think your idea is brilliant."

"Let me show you what I have in mind then. Come on, let's hurry."

CHAPTER 37

W e each put away our Christmas gifts the next day and completed the odd chores accompanying traveling and returning home. I gathered the laundry, and as I searched the pockets before putting clothes into the washer, I remembered the ticket I had found in Mike's pocket a few weeks earlier from the jewelry store in Santa Fe. I wondered about it for a moment and then pushed it aside. It couldn't have been that important.

Romano and Randy had invited just the three of us for dinner to celebrate New Year's Day—Mike, Isabella, and me. Mimi was away, as were Cal and Virginia. We wouldn't dress for dinner; we had been advised to come casual. Before leaving for Santa Fe, I had bought champagne and chocolate truffles, which I was taking for dessert. I knew our dinner would be outstanding no matter what Romano cooked, and I salivated just thinking about it.

While shopping in Santa Fe, I bought Romano and Randy a beautiful handwoven throw in colors that matched their décor. It was an exquisite work with a delicate texture and feel—warm and inviting. I knew it would be perfect for throwing around Randy as he sat watching television or reading. Although Romano never seemed to sit still long enough to need it, it was big enough for the two of them if he sat next to Randy.

Sweet Pea had also been invited, which was good since she was still spooked from all the fireworks the night before. As we waited outside their house, my heart lifted as the door opened, and Randy greeted us with genuine joy at seeing us. I immediately inspected him to see if his cast had been redone and made smaller. Instead of it being exposed, his pants covered his cast. That meant the doctors thought his leg had healed enough to have his cast refitted to give him greater mobility.

Delicious aromas greeted us, and my stomach rumbled with anticipation. I was not the only one eager to partake in Romano's cooking as we watched Sweet Pea take off and race toward the kitchen.

Randy laughed, "C'mon in. Sweet Pea already knows where 'her bread is buttered.' Smart dog."

Romano came to greet us with Sweet Pea dancing at his feet. Later, as we sat seeping our cocktails, Isabella asked to be excused. She headed into the kitchen for privacy to call her girlfriends. I was happy to have her out of the way while we told Romano and Randy about Redmond's death. I knew Isabella was sad about what happened to Redmond despite what he had put her through when he kidnapped her. She was learning firsthand what a horrible disease addiction was, which was something to discuss with her therapist.

"So what do you think, Mike?" asked Randy. "Was his death more than suicide?"

"Yeah, I think so. Once you get involved with thugs, as Redmond did, it's easy to question what seems too obvious. We have to wait for the coroner's report, and then we'll see. I feel sorry for Coyote because he feels responsible like we all do when we haven't been able to save someone from their own choices."

"Yes, there is that," said Randy, who became thoughtful. Isabella entered the room, and Romano got up to hand her a large present wrapped in beautiful paper with a full red bow. "Santa left this for you, Isabella."

"For me? Really?" she smiled as she held out her arms to take the present from him. "What is it?"

He patted her head and said, "I think you'd better open it to see."

She turned to me and smiled. She sat on the floor, carefully peeled the paper away, and lifted the top of the box to peek inside. "Oh, it's beautiful!" she cried as she lifted a stunning designer soft-leather backpack. "Thank you, Romano and Uncle Randy! I love it!"

I knew how much that cost, and to say it was an extravagance was an understatement. I eyed Romano, who mouthed to me over Isabella's head, "I got it on sale," as if that made it okay.

I reached for the gift we had brought and handed it to Randy to open while Romano adjusted the backpack straps to fit Isabella. Randy waited until he finished, then together, they opened the gift. As Randy shook out the throw, they both oohed and aahed. "The colors are perfect! And it's so soft."

Randy threw it around them both, and we watched as they kissed. "Thank you so much."

Next, Romano handed me an envelope with Mike's and my name written across it. I opened it and removed the card, giving it to Mike to read. Inside was a weekend pass to an exclusive Brentwood, California club I'd only recently learned about.

"Romano and Randy, you shouldn't have. That's way too much," I protested.

"The owner is a friend of ours," said Randy. "You two need a quiet weekend away, and you'll fall in love with this place. And the food is divine, isn't it, Romano?"

He patted his stomach. "For sure."

I kissed them both while Mike clapped them on the shoulder. "Thank you so much."

Dinner was elegant in its simplicity—Salmon filets, fresh imported peas with mint, and baked stuffed potatoes. Cranberry pie and the truffles I brought finished the meal. Then a New Year's champagne toast was given.

Romano asked Isabella what she wanted for the upcoming year, and her words humbled us all. "I want my family to be safe."

That night, as I lay by Isabella's side, I asked, "Do you worry about your family's safety, Isabella? Do you worry about your family in Mexico?"

"Sometimes."

"If you ever want to visit them to make sure they're okay, I'll do my best to arrange that …."

"It's not them that I'm concerned about," interrupted Isabella. "I'm worried about you."

"Me? Why, my darling girl, nothing is going to happen to me," I consoled. "Besides, with you and Mike to save me, there's nothing to fear, right?"

"Mama, you're going to have to be careful," she said, looking me in the eye.

"Okay, I promise to be more careful… honest," I vowed.
"Good."

"Try not to worry, okay, kiddo?"

She said nothing, and I wondered if she could also read my concern for her. It seemed so unfair that Isabella had reason to worry about her family being safe—here in Las Vegas, Santa Fe, and Mexico. The break-in had attacked our safety, and we knew things were in flux. I bent and kissed her goodnight and left with a heavy heart.

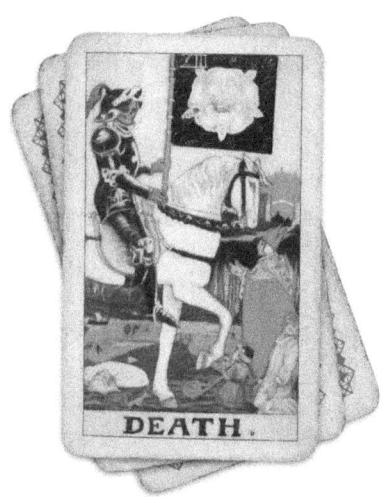

CHAPTER 38

T he following day, Isabella wasn't herself. She seemed hesitant about going to school. "Isabella, what's wrong?"

"Nothing, Mama."

"Isabella?" I coaxed.

"Do you think Tiffany will still be going around telling lies about me?"

"I don't know. I know both headmistresses are working to clear up Tiffany's false statements. But no matter what, you know the truth, and the truth always comes out… sometimes not as quickly as you may want. Keep in mind that the only person you have control over is you. So go on your way, and don't let Tiffany bother you. If you need to talk or take a break, go to the headmistresses' offices."

"Okay, Mama. Anyway, Sammy will be there. I will ask him if he wants to come home with me tomorrow."

"Good idea."

Mike came into the kitchen with his hair damp from the shower. "You two look serious. What am I missing?"

"Nothing," said Isabella as she hugged Mike goodbye and raced to the school bus.

"That girl of ours has a lot on her mind, what with Tiffany spreading lies about her. Now, there's the break-in here at the house too. She will ask Sammy to come home with her tomorrow, and I hope that works out for her. I'm curious to meet him, aren't you?"

"Yeah, I am. I certainly hope he's a better friend to her than Tiffany."

I nodded. "When did you say Brian would be here to stay with us for a few days?"

"Not until next week. Brian's going to help me with the new assignment then."

"It'll be nice to have him here. He seemed a little distracted in Santa Fe."

"The Christmas holidays are always tough for him because of his sister's death at that time of year, but he snaps out of it after a few days."

"Suicide is always sad."

"Yes, it is. Well, I guess I'd better be off to work. Are you going to check out things at the construction site?"

"Yup. Since Romano was the only one around to keep an eye on things, he will meet me there and point out what has been done while we were in Santa Fe."

"Sounds good. Keep in touch, and lock up when you leave, hear?" Mike ordered.

Instead of his words ruffling my feathers as his ordering me about had previously done, I'd learned that Mike tended to be that way when he was afraid for me. I nodded and leaned into him to kiss him goodbye with fervor.

He pulled me closer and whispered playfully in an English accent into my ear, "You light my fire, baby." He stepped back far enough to kiss me thoroughly on the lips. His cell phone chirped, and he turned away to answer it. As he headed to the door, he said, "Work calls. Just be careful, and don't get into trouble, hear?"

I tried to push away my unease at his words and returned to the kitchen to clean up the dishes before I left to meet Romano.

Climbing out of my car and viewing the construction site, I was amazed at what had been accomplished while I'd been in Santa Fe. With the roofing nearly completed and the windows and doors in place, things looked buttoned up. Most of what was going on now was the "finish work" inside, with various sub-contractors doing their thing. I was excited to see how both buildings fit into the plot of land without crowding each other. They were going to be beautiful, especially Romano's restaurant. He still hadn't named it yet.

The most exciting and fun part for Romano and me was selecting paint colors, fixtures, bathroom pieces, kitchen cabinets, sinks, tile, carpet, etc. Romano had other decisions to ensure everything flowed smoothly in the commercial kitchen. I knew he and Randy had spent the past few days finalizing their choices. Before leaving for Santa Fe, I met with the designer to finish the last few things. Mimi had politely stepped away from being involved with Romano's and my choices, saying it was up to us. She was curious to see what we'd chosen, though.

I heard Romano and Randy approach from behind, and I turned and smiled as they came closer. While I waited for them, Red, the former site manager we'd had dismissed from overseeing our project, stepped out of the restaurant building and headed toward us.

"Where's Eddie?" I asked.

"Not here. Why?"

"I have some things I want to go over with him. When is he due back?"

"He's sick. You're going to have to deal with me," he sneered … "or not."

Romano and Randy approached with helmets and handed me one while they put on theirs. "Where's Eddie?" asked Romano.

"What are you, an echo or something?" asked Red.

Romano eyed me. "He's sick, so we have to work through Red," I said.

"Oh. Well, let's go in, and I'll show you what's been happening," Romano said as he placed his hand on Randy's shoulder to guide him inside.

"Oh, no, you don't. No visitors are allowed while my crew is working. You'll have to come back later."

"No way, Red. We're here now, going in," I retorted. "C'mon, Romano and Randy, let's check things out." The three of us headed inside, followed by a disgruntled Red. Everyone inside was busy, and plumbers were hooking up the bathrooms' sinks, toilets, and cabinets. "Let's make sure everything is correct," I said, heading to where the plumbers worked.

A cool-looking sink was the length of the wall with separate spouts poured into the single basin and drain. It was made of copper and was stunning. The same sink had been installed in the Ladies' bathroom, too. Romano's smile said it all.

Then, Romano led me into the kitchen, where sheetrock hung on the walls and was being taped by two workers on stilts. Before any appliances and cabinets were installed, this area would be transformed with paint and tile. Then, we entered the main dining room, which was open with a cathedral ceiling exposing cherry wooden beams. A special sound-diminishing foam would be installed between the beams, considerably cutting down the customer noise and giving it a more intimate atmosphere.

I couldn't contain myself. "Romano! I love it! Your restaurant is going to be spectacular!" Both Romano and Randy beamed.

"Let's go see what's happening at your building," suggested Randy.

After making our way to the building that would house the non-profit agency handling human trafficking, I was disappointed that it wasn't nearly as far along as the restaurant's building. A single workman was fiddling with venting for the air conditioner and heating system. Both buildings were to be completed simultaneously, and I wondered if that was possible.

"Not much to see right now," I said.

"I know you're disappointed. Just wait a day or two. That'll change," Romano said, patting my shoulder.

We left out the side door of the building instead of the front. As I lowered myself to the ground on the rickety temporary stairs, I saw beer bottles sprawled further away. I called to Romano, "Look at this!" I went closer and kicked at the empty bottles. Was Jerry spending time here? Were the guys drinking on the job? We didn't need that going on.

"C'mon," I said. Let's find Red."

Romano, Randy, and I left to search for him, only to discover that he'd already packed up and left for the day to check on another site where he was in charge. Mimi was due back the next day, and we'd take it up with her then. It seemed there was always some problem to discuss with her, which bothered me. She had enough on her hands, what with her father being so ill.

CHAPTER 39

I hurried through the grocery store, making sure I didn't leave out items I knew we needed. It was too easy for me to get caught up in viewing every-thing for sale, wanting to try anything new. I needed to be home when Isabella returned from school so that I wouldn't allow her to worry about me. She was under enough stress at school.

Later, as I was stowing away the last of my purchases, I heard Isabella pound her way up the front walk. Sweet Pea barked, and with her tail wagging, she ran to the door to greet Isabella. Suddenly, the door flung open. Instead of stopping to say hello, Isabella ran right past us and up the stairs to her bedroom. Sweet Pea raced after her, and I followed, wondering what had happened. When I reached Isabella's bedroom, she had all the drawers of her chest open and was plowing through them, searching for something.

"What's wrong, Isabella? What are you looking for?"

"Mama, where is the blue sweater you bought me before we left for Santa Fe?"

"It should be inside your drawer—the one you have open. Isn't it there?"

"No, and neither is the one with flowers that Virginia knit for me." She squinted her eyes and pursed her mouth in determination and anger. "I know who broke into our house."

"You do?"

"Yes, it was Tiffany! She was wearing my blue sweater at school today. I know it was mine. She even asked me if I liked her new sweater. I hate her, Mama! I do," Isabella proclaimed as tears rolled down her face.

My heart fell. I knew Tiffany wouldn't have been alone if she had broken into our house. Two sets of dishes were used. Who had been with her? I hurried to Isabella and wrapped her in my arms. "Oh, I'm so sorry, Isabella. Did you tell anyone else about this?"

"Only Sammy and he confirmed it was Tiffany who broke into our house and that someone else was with her, but he doesn't know who."

I rose and silently handed Isabella a Kleenex before I sat down again on the bed beside her. I put my arm around her as she sniffled into the tissue. "I need to talk to Mike about this. We can't accuse Tiffany of breaking into our house without proof."

"But, Mama, we know.... "

"Isabella, we don't have proof. Your blue sweater is classic and not unique. Anyone could have one like it. However, the sweater that Virginia made for you is a different story. We'll have to wait and see if she dares to wear it to school."

"Why is Tiffany so mean to me, Mama?" sniffed Isabella.

"Remember when Redmond kidnapped you and Grandmother talked about him being in the shadows? If people aren't living their best lives, they live in the shadows."

"But Tiffany isn't like Redmond; she's not on drugs or anything," she protested.

"Sometimes, when we don't feel loved or feel 'less than,' we act out negatively. Think about Tiffany. She's always causing trouble just to get attention. Maybe she doesn't feel she gets enough of that at home. You've said that she's often left alone. That doesn't sound very loving to me, does it to you?"

"I guess not," she responded in a reluctant voice.

"It doesn't help to hate her either, Isabella. That's negative energy, which doesn't serve anyone well."

She nodded. "Okaay."

I kissed her and hugged her. "So tell me, is Sammy coming for dinner tomorrow?"

Isabella's face lit up. "Yes. Here's the telephone number to call his mother. You'll like him, Mama."

"If you do, I'm sure I will too."

I left Isabella while she put everything she'd pulled out back into her drawers. I went down to the office to make my call to Sammy's mother. As I dialed her number, I had no idea what to expect. I wondered what she thought about Sammy's intuitive abilities. She picked up right away.

"Hello, this is Rosalie Bennett …"

"Oh, yes! Sammy said you'd be calling," she enthused. "He talks about Isabella all the time. I'm so pleased he's made a friend. It isn't always so easy for him. Oh, my name is Maggie, by the way." She chuckled. "You'll have to excuse me. My husband tells me I can say more in 5 seconds when it takes most people 60."

I laughed. "Hi, Maggie. We'd love Sammy to take the bus home with Isabella tomorrow and have him stay for dinner. We can drive him home around 8 o'clock if that's okay with you?"

"That sounds wonderful. I'm so glad that Sammy and Isabella are friends. He says that she has the gift, too. How exceptional our children are, don't you agree?"

"Yes, I do. Special in so many ways."

"That's for sure," chuckled Maggie. "Thanks for Sammy's invite. I know he's looking forward to it."

After I ended the call, I considered the difference between Tiffany's mother and Sammy's. Maggie sounded so down-to-earth and pleasant. It would be interesting to meet Sammy.

CHAPTER 40

I tossed and turned in my sleep enough to disturb Mike as well. By dawn, I think he was as glad as I was to end the struggle for sleep. "Lord, woman, what got into you last night? Still bothered about Tiffany?"

"I kept having dreams where I was running after her to give her a piece of my mind. She kept eluding me, and I could never catch her. Right now, I feel as if I've run a marathon." I noticed the bags under Mike's eyes and said, "I'm so sorry I kept you awake."

"Yeah, well, I hope you're not too tired to kiss me."

I moved closer and placed my head on his shoulder. "Never for you."

After he gave me a long, warm kiss, he tightened his arm around me, pulling me further against him. "I don't know what we're going to do about Tiffany. We can't arrest her now; we know she wasn't alone. We found a cigarette butt outside. Although we forgot to set the alarm, the door was pried by someone who knew his way around it. Someone experienced."

"So, what are we going to do?" I asked.

"Let's see if she wears the sweater that Virginia made for Isabella. That'll give us some concrete evidence—not that she broke in here, but that she's wearing a piece of stolen property."

"That girl is nothing but trouble," I lamented. "Let's hope that this Sammy is a different story."

"Yes," Mike agreed.

A knock at the bedroom door alerted us that it was time to start the day. It was evident by Isabella's looks that she hadn't slept well either.

Mike said, "So today is the day we meet Sammy."

Isabella smiled. "Yup, it is."

"Okay, then. I'd better get up and fix my ladies some breakfast."

Isabella snuggled against me. "Mama?"

"What, sweetie?"

"What should I do if Tiffany wears the sweater that Virginia made for me to school today?"

"Excuse yourself from class and talk to one of the headmistresses. After you leave for school, I will call them and let them know what's happening. Maybe you could have Sammy take a picture of her on his cell phone."

"Okay, Mama."

"C'mon, let's get dressed and start our day."

The day flew by. I'd spoken to both headmistresses, so they knew what'd happened. I ran down to the construction site to check on things. Again, only one man was at my building working on the HVAC system. He said he'd be finished by late the next day, and things would begin rolling along. I wrote another article for Women Living Well magazine on trust. As I was writing, I realized that was what I needed—faith that things would work out—hopefully, the way I wanted.

I became engrossed in what I was doing, so when I heard Sweet Pea bark, I was surprised to realize it was time for the school bus to arrive. As I headed into the kitchen, I heard loud laughter coming through the front door that'd been flung open.

"Mama?"

"I'm in the kitchen, Isabella."

Isabella was first to enter with flushed cheeks and brown eyes sparkling. She reached behind her and pulled Sammy forward. He was not much taller than her, with his coloring opposite hers. He had blond hair, freckled light skin, and a startling, handsome face with two huge eyes staring at me—one blue and one brown. He held his hand out for me to shake, "Hi, Msthes Bennett," he lisped.

"Why, hello, Sammy. It's nice to meet you."

"Thanksth."

"Sammy, your eyes are beautiful. Did you know that means that you're special? Some say that the fairies have touched you."

He blushed. "The kidsth are always teasing me about it, but I don't care. I know things about them that they don't know I know."

"Well, there is that. Isabella says that you're a Seer."

He nodded and smiled as Isabella handed him a cold can of fizzy fruit water.

"What do you want to do?" she asked him.

"Let'ths do our homework so we can play the Xsth Box later." He bent down to pat Sweet Pea. "C'mere, girl. She's so cute."

Sweet Pea danced around him like she used to do with Brian. The dog was taken with this handsome, unusual boy.

"I'll start dinner soon. Is there anything you can't eat, Sammy?"

"No, the chicken you have in mind will be fine."

Surprised, all I could say was, "Okay, then."

When Mike arrived home, I greeted him with a kiss. He pulled me tight to him and murmured, "Are you sure no quickies are allowed?"

We heard Isabella and Sammy coming down the stairs. "There's something I need to tell you about Sammy. He's a great mind reader, so watch what you're thinking," I teased as I removed his hands from my behind and stepped back from him. Isabella and Sammy entered the kitchen where we stood.

"This is Sammy," Isabella said to Mike.

"Hello, Sammy. How's it going?"

"Good. Sweet Pea needs to go out, though."

"Oh, okay," said Mike as we watched them heading to the sliding glass door. Mike turned to me and pointed to his eyes. I nodded, indicating that yes, indeed, I'd noticed them too. I shook my head at Mike teasingly, and he laughed.

The conversation at the table was impressive. It was apparent that Sammy was exceptionally bright. I could tell that Mike was taken with him.

"So, Sammy, what's your favorite subject?" asked Mike.

"Speech therapy. I'm learning to move my tongue differently when I thspeak so that I don't lispsth."

"Good for you; you'll do it," encouraged Mike.

He nodded. "I also like to write stories. Isthabella and I are writing one together."

"That's nice," I said. "What's it about?"

Isabella jumped in, "We want to surprise you, don't we?" she asked Sammy.

"Sure," he responded to the apparent new twist in the plan.

The meal was enjoyable and relaxing. When we finished, I said, "You two, go ahead, and I'll clean up. Mike and I will sit here with our wine for a while."

Sammy rose from his seat and gathered his dishes, then Mike's, while Isabella gathered hers and mine to carry to the kitchen sink. Mike raised his brows at me while I smiled with approval. What a difference between having Tiffany here for dinner and Sammy.

"Did Tiffany wear Isabella's sweater to school today?" asked Mike when we were alone.

"No, she didn't wear the blue one either. I called the headmistresses and told them what had happened at our house. They said they would keep a close eye on Tiffany. Things aren't going as they'd hoped in their discussions with her. So the saga continues."

"Too bad. When is Mimi due back?"

"She should be arriving tonight."

"And what about Cal and Virginia?"

"Sometime this week."

"Lots going on, isn't there?"

I rose from the table and kissed the top of Mike's head. "I'd better clean up these dishes because it's almost time to drop Sammy home. Do you want to come with us?"

"I'd like to meet his parents. I'll drive. Just let me know when you all are ready."

Sammy lived in a housing development near us and rode the same school bus as Isabella each morning and after school. As we pulled into his driveway, the front door opened, and both of Sammy's parents stood framed in the doorway. Then together, they walked down to meet us. I smiled as I heard Maggie begin to talk to us before she was halfway to the car.

"Hi, there! I'm Maggie, and this is my husband, David. Did things go alright?" She peered into the back seat with its window open. "Hi, there! You must be Isabella. What a beauty you are!"

"Mom!" Sammy said in a scolding manner.

"I'm sorry. I hope I didn't embarrass you, Isabella." She shook her head and smiled. "Good."

David and Mike shook hands and chatted as Maggie opened the door for Sammy to get out. She looked through the opened door to where I sat. "I'm so glad to meet you, Rosalie. I've heard so much about you from what Isabella shares with Sammy. I remember you from when you stopped that terrible human trafficking scheme ...."

"Mom!"

"Sorry, I know I talk too much," she apologized. "C'mon, Sammy, let's get inside. It's cold out here,"

Sammy's father said. "So nice to meet you, folks." He held out his arms to gather Sammy and Maggie.

"We'll have you over here for dinner soon, Isabella," Maggie called out as she hunched her shoulders from the cold and joined Sammy and David to huddle as a group toward the open front door.

I laughed as soon as they were inside, and Mike and Isabella joined in. What a crazy family. I loved them!

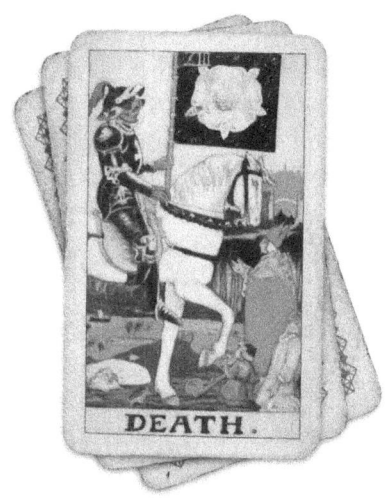

CHAPTER 41

A fter Isabella left for school and Mike went to the office, I hopped into the car to meet Mimi and Romano at the job site. I couldn't wait to see the expression on Mimi's face when she saw how far along the restaurant had come since she'd been here last. I knew Romano was looking forward to showing it off. There was talk about a grand opening in time for Mother's Day in May, but it depended upon a few things out of his control. However, he and Randy had already met with a few people they wanted to bring on board. That'd be the most challenging part—getting the staff set.

When I arrived on-site, I was the first one there. Red came stalking out of the restaurant building as soon as I pulled in. "What do you want?"

Impulsively, I asked, "How do you know Jerry?"

"What are you talking about?" he scowled.

"I saw you with Jerry the other day when he was passed out on the street. You were there. How do you know him?"

"None of your business," he snapped.

"Believe it or not, I do care about the man ...."

"Save your breath. I know all about what you did to Jerry."

"I didn't do anything to him!" I protested. "He needs help!"

"So what are you going to do about that, huh?" he challenged.

"What's going on?" Mimi asked as she came closer.

Red glared at us. "Don't bother the men, understand?" Red ordered and turned away.

I lifted my shoulders. "I asked Red how he knew Jerry, Jeff's former police partner."

"The one who tried to hurt you? Oh, I thought I told you. My Dad said that they're cousins."

"Cousins? Really?"

Mimi nodded as Romano joined us. His face glowed with pride as he spread his arms wide, "Well, Mimi, what do you think? Just wait until you see how the beams turned out in the cathedral ceiling."

"I can't wait," she said, grabbing his arm and letting him lead her inside.

I followed, lost in thought. If Red and Jerry were cousins, was he involved with Jerry leaving the girls' bones on the job site? Did he know who murdered them? Was he involved with any of the recent killings? Although he was unsavory, I couldn't picture Red as a murderer. I was pretty sure the older murders had something to do with the former chief of police, but the newer ones? I had no idea.

"Hey, Rosie, are you coming?" hollered Romano.

"Yep, I'll be right there."

Mimi loved what'd been done so far, from the kitchen and bathroom sinks to the dining room with its cathedral ceiling. After she finished her tour, I turned to the two of them. "What are you going to name the restaurant?"

Mimi and Romano looked at one another with a flash of understanding. Romano spoke up, "We haven't decided."

"Well, whatever you choose, I'm sure it'll be wonderful."

"I see more workmen in your building, Rosie," said Romano.

"Thank God," I said as we headed there.

It didn't take nearly as long to inspect the office building, and it wasn't as much fun because everything was pretty basic. The decorating would make it more unique, and I had a lot of ideas for that.

When we finished, Romano and Mimi excused themselves to tend to other things, and I climbed into my car to head home. I purposely drove by the plot that would hold Tony's new gentlemen's club. I was surprised to see the land staked out, outlining the proposed building. It looked huge. It was an enigma to me how Tony had gotten away with all that mess at the Purple Passion Lounge— and the same for Johnny.

I returned home, and knowing it'd soon be time for Isabella to return home from school, I took Sweet Pea for a walk. Once home, I thought having a cup of hot cocoa waiting for Isabella would be nice since it was cold outside. As I was preparing it, I heard the squeaky brakes of the school bus pull in and then out of the driveway. Oddly, I didn't hear Isabella running up the front steps as usual. I went to the front door and looked out. There she was— wiping away tears— sitting on the lowest front step. She looked up, and seeing me standing in the doorway, she straightened up, trying to put on a brave face.

"What's wrong?" I asked as I took a step down toward her. I gathered her into my arms. "C'mon. Let's go inside. I have hot cocoa waiting for you."

"Mama, I hate her. I can't help it. I hate her!" she said as she burst into fresh tears.

I pulled Isabella along into the kitchen. "What's happened? Tell me."

Through snuffles, Isabella said, "Today, Tiffany had on the sweater that Virginia made me. I told her that she'd stolen my sweater, and I wanted it back." She bowed her head. "I know you said to go to the headmistresses, but I was just so mad."

I nodded. "So, what happened?"

"She called me a liar. She said she didn't steal the sweater; it was a gift. Then she said …" New tears stopped her from going on.

"What did she say," I asked softly, patting her shoulder.

"She… she… she called me a 'Beaner' and told everyone no one wanted me… that I was a ward of the state. She said I belonged in Mexico, and her mother would have me kicked out of the school." She placed her head down on the table and sobbed her heart out.

I was furious! And where were the headmistresses in all this? Why was I finding this out now? My cell phone rang, and when I saw it was the school calling, I had to bite my tongue before calmly saying, "Hello."

"Oh my, Rosie. I apologize. We had every intention of calling you before now, and certainly, before Isabella got home, but we've had our hands tied, what with dealing with Tiffany and her mother. I'm so sorry."

"I'm distraught to learn what I have from Isabella. I'd like to hear what you say about the situation."

"Of course. What has Isabella told you so far?"

I relayed what I knew, and I heard Dorothy sigh heavily. "Yes, that's all true. We separated the girls this morning, and it wasn't until the afternoon that this all happened. Tiffany called her mother and told her that Isabella had threatened her. Her mother called the police to come to the school to 'protect her daughter' until she could get there. As you can imagine, it's been a terrible afternoon."

"What is wrong with that woman?"

Dorothy sighed. "A lot, although I shouldn't have said so."

"So, what happens now?"

"We've asked Tiffany's mother for a family meeting with all three. The meeting will occur tomorrow or the day after, depending on Tiffany's father's schedule. We've also asked to have the two sweaters brought in at that time. Tiffany's mother doesn't want Tiffany to return to school until after the meeting." Dorothy sighed. "I must warn you. I think she's trying to use some pull to have Isabella removed from school."

"Why is that woman so hateful?" I asked, holding back the tears that threatened. An idea began to form. "Can I call you back?" I'd want to discuss it with Mike and Isabella first.

"Of course."

I hung up the phone and waited for Mike to come home.

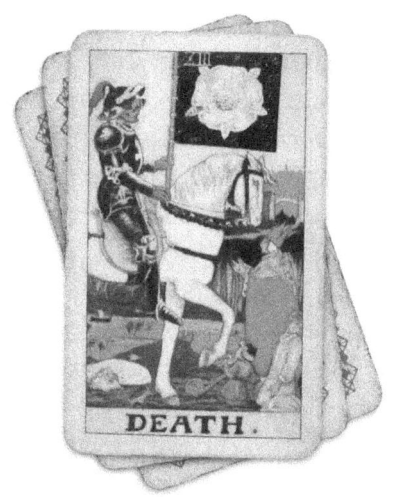

CHAPTER 42

I awoke excited but nervous. Mike and I had discussed what I wanted to do at length, and later, we'd included Isabella in our discussion. She agreed it could make a difference and be helpful for everyone. Dorothy and Alicia thought my suggestion was stellar, so I would go to Isabella's school later to share my experiment with her class.

After I parked the car and walked inside the school, I went to where Dorothy and Alicia would meet me. With a video camera in hand, Alicia led me into the classroom. She'd be recording everything, so it would be available should any issue arise about what I said.

"Okay, class. Gather around. We've asked Isabella's mother to come in today to share what she's learned about energy. Pay close attention. It's inspiring. Please welcome her."

I began. "I'm delighted to be here today. Did you know that everything is energy? Every little thing? Even plants? Did you know how powerful you are by what thoughts you have and what words you use when speaking to each other and even plants?"

I went on to explain how this experiment by Dr. Emoto would work. I took out two look-alike plants and two jars of sealed water with rice from my bag. Since it was a small class, I had each person come up and write a negative word on one of the jars and a positive one on the other jar. Then I had each student come up and read aloud the word they'd written on the positive jar, and then we went through it again with the negative one. Each day, I want you to go to each jar and think about and repeat aloud the word you've written. Does anyone know what will happen in a few days?"

"I do," said Sammy. The positive jar will be happy, and the negative one won't be."

"That's right. And you will be able to see the difference, won't you, class?"

Heads nodded. "So, let me ask each of you this? How did you feel when you told the jar that you didn't like it?"

A few students looked down, while the others looked lost in thought. I walked to the flip chart and reached for one of the many-colored markers. "This is the color for saying anything negative or hurtful to someone or something." I drew two heads of a person, and above each, I filled in a scribbled cloud with black. I repeated it for the jar of rice. As I looked around the room, the kids' faces were solemn.

"Now, see what happens when you say something positive about someone or something." I drew two more faces, and in the cloud above each, I drew a rainbow with all the colors. I did the same for the jar of rice. Now the faces in the room staring back at me were happier. "You'll have a chance to see this for yourselves in a few days when you continue to talk to the plants and jars of rice."

One of the students yelled out, "Cool."

"Can anyone tell me how this works in the classroom?"

Tina's soft voice announced, "Be nice to each other, and no bullying."

"Yes, how we treat each other counts. Each time we accuse someone of something or say things that aren't true can hurt a person and take away their color. For both the speaker and the receiver, right?"

"Are you here because of what Tiffany said about Isabella?" asked one of the older girls.

"In part," I admitted. "I also know how important it is to remember how negative words can hurt someone. And it's easy to remember that whatever you say to another person, you will know whether it's good or bad just by how you feel. Pretty simple, don't you think?"

"What do you do if someone threatens to beat you up if you don't do what she says?" asked a different girl.

Alicia stood and said, "You come to me."

"Any other questions?" I asked.

"Is Isabella a ward of the state like Tiffany said?" asked a third girl.

"I'm her legal mother, so she is my daughter, like being adopted. But she has family back in Santa Fe, too." I laughed. "She has lots of family with all her aunts, uncles, cousins, and sister-friends."

"Sister-friends? What's that?" asked Deborah.

"When you're more like sisters than friends," said Isabella.

"Can I be your sister-friend?" she asked.

"Me, too," said several other girls.

Isabella looked at me in slight alarm, not knowing what to say. I smiled at Alicia, who grinned back. Not a bad problem to have.

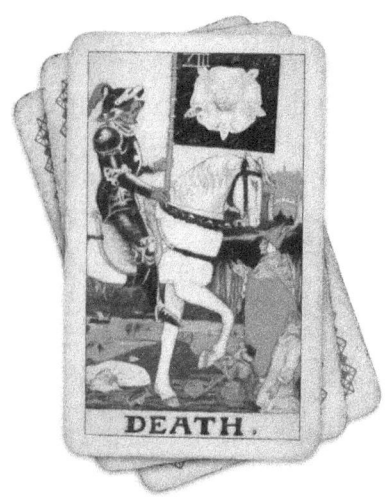

CHAPTER 43

T he following day, I smiled as I watched Isabella rush to get on the school bus—something much different than previous days. Sammy waved to her to join him, and she practically danced to where he sat. I was relieved to know that things would be better for Isabella at school, especially since she now had some classmates who wanted to be her friend.

Virginia was back in town and wanted me to help her pick out carpet and paint colors for her new place. She and Cal had ordered stainless steel appliances for the kitchen and laundry room, and as the landlord, Cal was paying for everything. I was thrilled for her.

I dashed out of the house to meet Virginia, and as I loaded into the car, I heard the house phone ringing. I decided to ignore it. All my close friends and associates had my cell phone number if they wanted to contact me, so, most likely, it was a sales call. When I reached the store where I was to meet Virginia, I forgot all about it.

The day was filled with us matching paints to carpets, looking at different new furniture, and all the things everyone wanted when starting a new stage of their life. I filled Virginia in on what'd happened with Isabella, and she was furious with Tiffany and her mother.

"They'll get back the pain they've given out; that's how life works," Virginia vowed.

After a leisurely lunch, I looked at my watch and realized I'd have to hustle to be home in time for Isabella. "So I'll see you tomorrow then, Virginia? I'll be going with Isabella to the soup kitchen for her volunteer work, and Brian will be arriving on Sunday to stay for a few days."

"Will Tiffany be there at the soup kitchen too? Aren't the two of them supposed to be separated?"

"I'm not going to have Isabella lose out because of Tiffany."

"I don't blame you. I'll see you tomorrow, then."

When I arrived home, seeing Isabella happy when she came through the door was a relief. "How was school today?"

"Good. Tiffany wasn't there," she laughed.

"Well, there's something to be said about that then, right?"

"Deborah asked me if I would be at the soup kitchen tomorrow. I said that I wasn't sure but that I thought so. Right, Mama?"

"Yes, we'll both be there for sure."

"Good. I'll let Deborah know and then call Nica and Angela."

"Okay. Don't forget that Uncle Brian is coming on Sunday to stay with us for a few days. So please make sure that the bathroom is picked up before then."

"Okay, Mama. Come on, Sweet Pea."

Mike walked through the door, surprising me. "You're home early," I said.

"Yes. The end of a long week. The body we found buried in the desert isn't the missing girl I'm searching for, which doesn't surprise me. I have a feeling she's alive somewhere, hiding. I hope I find her soon."

"I know you're worried about her," I said as I went to him and rested my palm against his cheek. Looking deep into his eyes, I said, "You'll find her; I know you will."

He pulled me closer and said in a husky voice, "Ahh, my queen." He bent down lower and kissed me thoroughly, molding me against him. "I think we need to do something about that no quickies rule," he whispered. As we heard Isabella and Sweet Pea coming down the stairs, he said, "Or not."

I laughed. "I guess we'll have to work that out."

Isabella came rushing to us. "When I called Deborah about tomorrow, she asked me if I'd heard about Tiffany."

"What about her?" I asked, dread filling me.

"Deborah said that she's gone missing. She saw it on the news."

My face blanched. "Oh, no," I said and rushed into my office.

"What's wrong?" Mike asked as he and Isabella followed me. Sure enough, the telephone message light was blinking. With great trepidation, I pushed play. Goosebumps covered my body as I heard the message:

"This is Sheriff Taylor calling. Rosalie Bennett, please call me as soon as you can. It's an urgent matter. Here's my number. Thank you."

We looked at each other, wondering if this had something to do with Tiffany. "You'd better call him right away, Rosie," urged Mike.

I dialed the phone with shaking hands as Isabella and Mike stood glued in their spots. I put the phone on speaker so they could hear what the sheriff had to say. "Sheriff? My name is Rosalie Bennett returning your call. How may I help you?"

"Are you aware that Tiffany Ellison is missing?"

"My daughter just told me. When did this happen?"

"We don't know exactly. Mrs. Ellison believes it was sometime yesterday."

"What do you mean? Her mother isn't sure when Tiffany went missing?"

The sheriff coughed. "Before Mrs. Ellison left to meet up with some of her friends for dinner, the night before last was the last time she saw Tiffany. Before she went out today to meet her friends for lunch, Mrs. Ellison discovered Tiffany's bed hadn't been slept in."

"Are you saying that Tiffany's mother never saw her for almost two days?"

"Ms. Bennett, do you know where Tiffany is? Have you seen her?"

"No, I'm sorry, I haven't."

"How about your daughter? Has she seen or heard from Tiffany?"

"She's here with me now and says she hasn't."

"I understand that there have been problems between your daughter and Tiffany. Mrs. Ellison says that your daughter threatened Tiffany. Do you believe that has anything to do with Tiffany's appearance?"

"I believe that you are listening to information that isn't true—especially when you consider the source. I don't believe you could've missed that Mrs. Ellison is a vindictive, selfish person who cares more about herself than her daughter!" I sputtered.

"Now, now. We're not here to judge. Will you promise to call me if you or your daughter hear from Tiffany? From what I've gathered, Tiffany spent a fair amount of time with you all, and she may reach out to you if she needs to."

"Of course, we'll call you immediately if we hear from her, Sheriff. Is there anything else you can tell us about what may have happened?"

"No, that's it. Here's my number again. Thank you for your time."

I hung up the telephone and looked at Isabella and Mike, who looked as stunned as me. "Let's hope this is just one of Tiffany's little pranks to get even with her mother," I grumbled.

"Mama, where could Tiffany be?"

"And who with?" added Mike.

"I don't have a clue," I answered. Without saying a word, the three of us hugged together.

"Poor Tiffany," said Isabella, upset not to have answers.

I heard my grandmother whisper, "Be patient. Visions come in their own time."

I'd learned that what she said was true. So at this point, it was a waiting game.

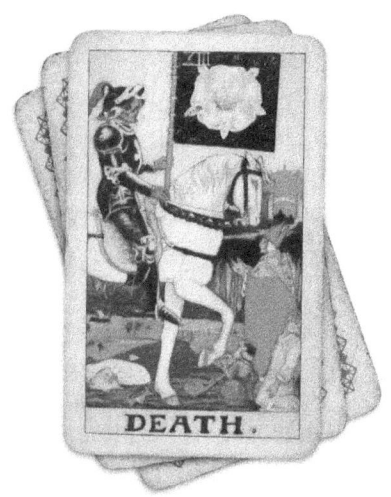

CHAPTER 44

A fter a restless night, I awoke to Mike stirring beside me, lost in a dream. I watched his facial expressions change to match whatever he was sorting out. Mike's unguarded, sleepy, boyish looks tugged at my heart, and I realized I'd grown to love him without limit. I knew he hadn't had an ideal childhood by any stretch of the imagination. He'd been left on his own a lot—like Tiffany in some ways. If he were Tiffany, where would he go?

He must have felt me studying him. His eyes opened, and he reached forward and smoothed my brow with his thumb. "You look upset. What's wrong?" Then as the realization came to him, he said, "You're not responsible, you know. Don't take that on. Tiffany's probably home by now, anyhow."

"I don't think so. I think this is far from over. We'll have to wait and see, won't we?"

"I'll check in with the police chief and see if he's working with the sheriff. Roberto will tell me what's going on."

"Thanks, Mike." I moved closer. We slowly explored each other's bodies with kisses until I moaned with pleasure, and it became urgent not to delay our becoming one.

Later, as I was dressing, Isabella wandered into the bedroom, "Where can Tiffany be?"

"I don't know. So far, I haven't received any visions, have you?"

She shook her head. "Not yet."

"Until then, we must continue our daily routines."

"Yeah, I guess so. Can Sammy come over later?"

"I don't see why not. Why don't you invite him to stay for dinner as well? Virginia is back, and she said Grandfather is due in today."

"Yes! I want Grandfather to meet him."

"I'll call Sammy's mother now, and then we'd better get ready to go to the soup kitchen."

By the end of my call, Virginia was downstairs waiting for her instructions. As intimacy heated up between her and Cal, we'd have to reconsider her role with us. It was going to be a bit awkward until then. By all accounts of their developing relationship, it appeared as if I would need to find myself a new housecleaner. And that was not always easy to find, or at least one that measured up to Virginia.

"Is Cal back yet?" I asked her.

"He'll be here in a few hours."

"If you didn't mind, I thought we'd all have dinner together tonight. Isabella's friend will join us. Does that fit in with your plans?"

"That sounds like the perfect solution. Cal was hoping to see you about something, anyway. Would you like me to make my chicken casserole that you all like?"

"That would be wonderful! I bought fresh fruit, which we can have for dessert, and salad mixings are in the refrigerator."

"If you need anything, text me, and after we're finished at the soup kitchen, I'll pick it up on my way home. Are you ready, Isabella?"

"Coming, Mama."

Nothing had changed in the few weeks we had been away from our volunteer work at the soup kitchen. People were still clustered together, lined up, waiting to get in. I looked to see if the two older men I didn't trust were there but couldn't find them.

When we got inside, Deborah greeted Isabella enthusiastically, and they took off to begin their chores. I dropped my jacket on the pile on a table and went to the front to help serve. Mabel was there, and she smiled at me. "What d'ya do? Leave trouble at home today, did ya?"

I pasted a smile on my face and nodded. I didn't know if I should say anything or not about Tiffany being missing, especially since I had no update. So I remained quiet.

The morning rolled along smoothly. The second man I didn't trust entered the door and got in line as we finished serving the food. When he stood before me, I asked, "Where's your friend?"

He stared at me and looked confused. Finally, he understood what I was asking. "Not here."

Ring a ding; you get the prize, I thought, annoyed. "Is he coming or not?"

"Naw, he's busy."

"Doing what?" I pushed.

He ignored me and walked away, plopping down at the far table. Mabel heard me and asked, "Is something the matter?"

"Sorry, I was curious to see if the other older man would also be coming in."

The second lady, who'd been serving the food, pulled up her empty bin to take into the kitchen, and Mabel began to do the same. I stepped from behind the serving counter and walked to where the older man was eating. "Have you seen Tiffany?"

He looked up at me with a toothless grin. "She's going to be a movie star; Thomas says so."

"Is Tiffany with him now?" I asked, alarmed at the thought.

"Dunno."

"Where does Thomas live?"

He looked puzzled. "The underground," he answered as if I were stupid.

"Where's that?" By this time, I had alarmed the man, and he suddenly pushed his empty plate away, ran to the front door, and went outside. He took off hurriedly, looking behind him to see if I'd followed.

Mabel had come back out front and had seen enough to make her ask in a concerned voice, "What's going on, Rosie?"

I explained about Tiffany being missing and what the older man had said. "Do you know where the underground is?"

"Oh, is that what Fred called it? He means the underpasses where many homeless sleep and sometimes cook. He might also have meant any empty buildings where the homeless have taken over. Stay away from them. Those places can be very dangerous."

I nodded as my heart pounded. I'd just had a quick vision of seeing Tiffany huddled in a corner in a dark, cold place. "Thanks, Mable. I'll keep that in mind."

When I returned to the kitchen, Isabella stood with the other girls, discussing what they wanted to cook for lunch the following week. Oh, poor Tiffany, I thought. Where are you?

As if I'd asked the question out loud, Isabella looked at me in puzzlement. "Mama?"

"I'm sorry to break this up, but it's time for us to go."

High fives made their round, and we were first out the door. "Did you see something, Mama?"

"Yes, did you?"

She nodded as we piled into the car and headed for home.

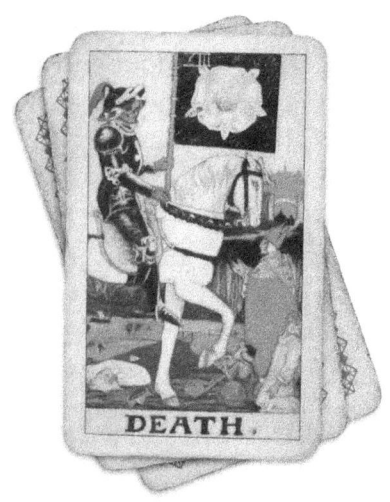

CHAPTER 45

A s we pulled into the house, I was relieved to see Mike's car was there, and he was home. When we got inside, I called, "Mike, where are you?"

He stepped out of the office. "Right here, Rosie, what's the matter?"

"We need to talk."

"Okay, c'mon in," he said, stepping aside.

"Come with me," I said, putting my arm around Isabella. We entered the office together and sat in the two club chairs facing Mike, who sat at my desk.

"What's up?" he asked with a furrowed brow. "What's wrong?"

"Both Isabella and I had visions of Tiffany huddled in a corner in a dark, cold place." I then explained what'd happened at the soup kitchen. "What should we do?"

He eyed the two of us with compassion. "The best thing you two can do is let the police do their thing. They're on it, and they have cops that know the places the older man was talking about. Allow them to see what they can do, okay? I don't want you to go out searching for Tiffany alone. Is that understood? Do you promise?"

Knowing Tiffany was alone, Isabella and I looked at each other, unsure whether we could commit to his wishes. Finally, I nodded. "Okay, I promise."

In a small voice, Isabella muttered, "Me too."

Mike looked relieved until I added. "I'll give them 24 hours."

Sweet Pea barked, announcing Cal's arrival. Instantly, Isabella rose and raced to the door to let him in, and we followed. She flung open the door. "Hi, Grandfather!"

I chuckled at Cal's surprised expression when he saw all of us crowded there to greet him. Then he smiled. "I can see that I've come to the right place. All my favorite people are here, including an exceptional dog," he said as he patted Sweet Pea on the head and held his arm open for Isabella to join him.

With smiles, we stood back and watched Isabella and Cal hug in welcome. Sweet Pea continued dancing around their feet.

"Sweet Pea, let Grandfather in," I commanded, and then Isabella bent to scoop up the dog.

We all entered the kitchen, where hot tea was steeping. Just as we were ready to sit down, we heard a car pull up, and Isabella raced to the door, hollering over her shoulder, "Sammy's here."

"Sammy?" asked Cal and Virginia together.

"Isabella's friend," I said. "He's quite special. Wait and see."

It was easy to see Isabella's excitement as she presented Sammy to Cal and Virginia. His eyes brightened with curiosity as Isabella introduced him to "my grandfather and his girlfriend."

I bit back a chuckle when Virginia's face turned bright pink upon hearing Cal remark, "That's right, she is. So, Sammy, how do you do?"

"I'm just fine, thank you."

"That's what I like to hear," Cal said. "We're lucky to be alive, aren't we?"

"Yes, but we never really die, you know. And you have …."

"Sammy?" I interrupted, sensing he was about to tell Cal his mother's spirit was around, "Would you like a hot cup of cocoa?"

He nodded, and Isabella, sensing the situation for what it was, pulled at him. "Let's get out some marshmallows, too."

They headed to the pantry while Virginia poured our tea. When we finished sipping it, Cal asked to speak with me alone. We left Virginia and Mike behind talking with Isabella and Sam about a school project they were doing. Once in the office, we sat in one of the club chairs and faced each other.

"What is it, Cal? What did you want to talk to me about?" I asked.

He reached for my hand and held it tight. "You have become very dear to me. I'm sure you must know how I feel about you—all of you. I think of you as my daughter."

"Yes, I feel the same."

"I've been talking to my accountant about starting a foundation in my mother's name—my birth mother's name. I think you know what happened to my mother and how fortunate I was to have my grandmother step in as my true mother to raise me. I don't remember much about my birth mother other than when I was young. She would visit me periodically, always making promises and never keeping them. It was always my grandmother who would straighten out my emotions and show me unconditional love. In much the same way, that's how she loved her daughter until the last time I saw my birth mother. My grandmother finally put her foot down and refused to let her see me again until she got clean and sober." His eyes softened with sorrow and watered. "Of course, that day never came."

I squeezed his hand. "I'm so sorry, Cal."

He continued. "It took me many years to understand that addiction is a maddening, destructive illness. One that my birth mother couldn't shake."

I nodded. "Look at how it ended for Coyote's poor nephew."

"Yes. That was sad... sadder for those left behind."

"A foundation in your birth mother's name sounds like a wonderful idea. What would it do?"

"Setting up a foundation is no easy task, and for it to succeed, there must be people at the helm to make it happen. That's where you'd come in, Rosie."

"Me? What do you mean?"

"I'm hoping you'd be willing to help me manage it and eventually take it over. There'd be a rather large salary for you for doing so."

"What exactly would I have to do?"

"I brought some papers for you to read about what it takes to set up a foundation and to keep it running. So read them, and talk it over with Mike before you give me an answer, okay?"

"I don't know what to say," I said, my mind whirling.

"Don't say anything yet. Take your time to think it over."

He stood up and pulled me to him in a fatherly manner. "As I said, I love you like a daughter, Rosie."

I kissed his cheek. "Does Virginia know about this?"

"As I'm sure you've noticed, our relationship is growing, so Virginia and I have talked a little about it. She knows I have some money, but I don't think she knows how much. I don't want that to interfere with our relationship. That is something I want to keep between us for now."

"I think Virginia is smitten with you, not your money," I protested.

His cheeks grew rosy. "Yes, I have to agree. However, Virginia does not need to know anything more now."

"Okay, mum is the word. And Cal? Thank you."

"Ahh, my dear, thank you for considering this," he said, eyes shiny with unreleased tears. Then, he turned away, leaving me in the office, lost in thought. I felt my grandmother's spirit around me.

"Oh, Gram, see what you brought into my life with your love and kindness all those years ago."

"Rosie girl, isn't life grand? One never knows where a single act of kindness can lead."

"What do you think I should do?"

"Whatever you want, sweetheart. Love you."

As I turned to leave, I bumped into my desk and stood mesmerized as I watched my tarot cards fall as if in slow motion. Goosebumps crossed my body as I watched them pile upon each other onto the floor. No surprise, the Death card sat on top, taunting me. Who was it going to be this time? Not Tiffany, I pleaded. And please, not Cal or anyone else I knew. Fate tossed its head and dared me to intervene.

CHAPTER 46

D inner was fun and a different story, with Sammy joining us rather than Tiffany. He was polite, witty, and uplifting, appreciating everything around him. I could see where it'd not always be easy for him to be accepted among his peers concerned with more mundane things. So I was surprised to learn that he was the star of his soccer team.

With Mike and Cal at the table, he soon became the center of attention and regaled them with stories about playing soccer. I watched Isabella's response, and if sensing me, she turned my way and smiled. It was apparent she was happy for him. She was such a beautiful soul, and my heart filled with love for her. How did I deserve this second chance to share a lifetime with her? I didn't know, but I was grateful we were together again this lifetime.

"Rosie? Earth to Rosie," Mike said.

"Sorry, my mind was far away. What?"

"May I pour you some more wine?"

"Yes, please. Virginia, thank you for making this casserole. It was so delicious, and there isn't a drop left," I said as I surveyed all the empty plates. "Are you ready for dessert, everyone?" I began to rise.

"No, Msthes Bennett. We've got thisth," Sammy said as he got up. And Isabella did the same, waving me back into my chair.

We remained at the table, relaxing and talking about the two missing girls—Tiffany and the one Mike was searching for—and the problem of human trafficking. Sammy and Isabella served the fruit and the cookies Virginia had made earlier. Then they passed on dessert, excusing themselves to play on the Xbox.

"No word from the sheriff or Roberto on the missing girls? I can't believe he and the other cops haven't found Tiffany yet. Can you call him?"

"Now? I'll call him first thing in the morning. I think Tiffany is stronger than you think, don't you, Cal?"

"There's something about her type that always seems to survive."

"What do you mean, her type?" I asked.

"She pushes the envelope if you know what I mean. Even flirting with Mike was a test. She doesn't know boundaries."

"Maybe because she doesn't have any," Virginia mumbled with disdain, obviously not a fan of Tiffany. The rest of us laughed in surprise because it was unusual for her to speak out negatively.

"Well, it's maddening to sit here doing nothing." Mike stirred in his seat, ready to speak. I held my hand up to stop him. "I know. I promised not to interfere for 24 hours."

"Longer than that, I hope," he said.

I remained quiet, and the energy in the room dropped. We all were worried.

Mike's phone buzzed with an incoming text. "Is everything okay?" I asked.

"Yeah. It's Brian. He will catch an earlier flight and be here tomorrow by 10 o'clock or so. He's texting me his flight info now."

Virginia rose. "Let me finish these dishes, so you young people can get to bed."

I was too tired to argue with her, and instead of doing them myself, I was more than grateful for her help.

Noting my fatigue, Cal offered, "We'll be happy to drop Sammy off at his house."

"That sounds wonderful. All of a sudden, I'm beyond tired."

"Stress," said Mike. "And worry."

A deep sense of foreboding filled me. Trouble was ahead, and I knew I'd be involved. I hoped a good night's sleep would help because I had no strength to deal with anything trying.

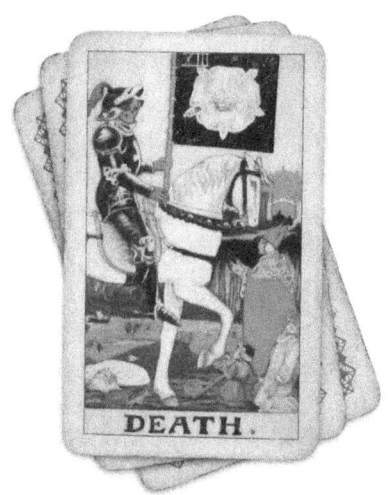

CHAPTER 47

When I awoke the following day, Mike's arm was around me in a spooning position. I stirred enough to make Mike groan and pull me tighter to him. I couldn't believe I'd slept through the night without getting up once.

"Is it morning already?" he asked in a sleepy voice.

I realized that as much as I felt under stress, he must feel the same. It wasn't that we felt responsible for Tiffany being missing; it was the fear that something terrible could happen to any young girl not wise enough to avoid disaster. As a Marine and now as a private detective, he'd seen enough to know the chances of anything good happening were slim for the two missing girls. And the longer the time, the worst the possibilities were.

I twisted in Mike's arms until we were face to face. "Hey, handsome, time to get up."

"Do I have to?" he teased in a laughing voice.

I chuckled. "That's the question all kids ask. The answer is 'Yes, you do, handsome.'"

"Not before you kiss me, though."

I nestled against his neck and then raised my face to seek out his waiting lips. Without warning, tears overflowed, and I reached up to wipe them away.

"What's the matter?" asked Mike rising on an elbow to look at me.

"Just happy to have you here with me."

"Oh, my beautiful queen," he moaned, crushing me against him. "How can you not know how much I love you and how happy I am to have you here with me?"

We held each other without words or movement, letting our soul energies meld. I'd never known or felt this sensation before. It stilled both of us in a way that was hard to explain. It was a wholeness that completed us, and I was overwhelmed by it. Mike was the first to move, looking deep into my eyes. "Wow, what was that?"

"Something beautiful," I whispered before our lips met. A knock on the door announced Isabella and Sweet Pea. "C'mon in," I said as Mike and I parted and sat up.

"Good morning, princess."

She smiled as she joined us on the bed, holding Sweet Pea in her arms. "When is Uncle Brian going to be here?"

"Sooner rather than later. I'd better get up and shower," I said.

"I'll go put the coffee on. Any takers for my scrambled eggs?"

"Yes, please," Isabella and I echoed.

"Give me 15 minutes, and I'll join you two," I said.

My mind fell into my worries, and I dressed in a pair of old jeans and a sweater that I wouldn't be upset if they got dirty. I envisioned myself and Isabella in a dark and filthy unfamiliar place. I shook my head to clear it, but the vision remained.

"Mama? The eggs are ready!" Isabella called upstairs.

"Coming."

When I walked into the kitchen, Mike was on the phone talking.

"Who's Mike talking to?" I asked Isabella.

"Roberto, I think. They're talking about Tiffany."

"Any news?"

She shrugged her shoulders. "I don't think so."

I poured a cup of coffee and sat down at the table. Mike was quiet as he served up the eggs and toast. "Any news, Mike?"

"Nope. They haven't found Tiffany yet," he replied, obviously disappointed. "I want you and Isabella to promise to stay put for another 24 hours and let the police do their job."

Isabella looked my way and gave me a slight shake of her head. I said, "Listen, we'll make a deal with you. We'll drive around and see if any visions come to us. If anything does, we'll call the police and let them take over."

"I don't like that at all. You always end up in the middle of things and get hurt. You've been lucky so far, so I wouldn't push it. I couldn't live with myself if anything happened to you—either of you."

"We'll be in the car and will be careful, I promise."

Mike's phone rang, pulling him away from our conversation. He returned to the table and said, "That's Brian. He's just landed, and I need to pick him up. You girls promise me you'll call the police if anything comes up, right?"

We both nodded, and he kissed Isabella on the top of her head and then came to me. "I love you, my queen. Remember that." He left in a hurry without finishing his eggs.

Isabella and I looked at each other. "Did you have another vision, Mama?"

I nodded. "Did you, too?"

She nodded. "In my vision was the creepy man who wants to make Tiffany a star."

"What exactly did you see?"

"He had her walking down the middle of some people, and they were laughing and hooting at her."

"What was she doing?"

Isabella lowered her eyes and mumbled, "Crying."

My heart lurched with sadness. "Okay, let's get in the car."

"Where are we going, Mama?"

"I have an idea of where to start looking, beginning with Jerry."

I grabbed a few bottles of water and some snacks. Then I went to my safe and loaded twenty dollar bills into my wallet to use as bribe money for answers to my questions. I tucked the wallet and cell phone into the inside pocket of my down jacket.

Isabella's cell phone buzzed. She looked at it and said, "It's Sammy."

"See what he wants."

Isabella listened, then said, "Let me ask my mother. Sammy knows we're up to something and wants to come too."

"He can't come with us. I don't want the responsibility. However, he can be our secret weapon and take part over the phone. How does that sound?"

After Isabella relayed that to Sammy, he seemed satisfied with his role in our search for Tiffany. It was lunchtime when so many homeless people shuffled out of their space, searching for something to eat. We said goodbye to Sweet Pea and loaded into the car.

I headed to where I'd seen Jerry passed out on the street. His "home" had to be close by, and I thought there might be a chance he'd be around.

When we came to the location I wanted, I slowed the car down, pulled to the side of the street, and waited. After 15 minutes without seeing him, I pulled into traffic and headed to the soup kitchen.

We pulled in and parked next to the soup kitchen. Lunch was over, and we saw several of the same people we'd seen yesterday come outside, including the woman I'd seen standing over Jerry when he had been passed out.

"Stay here, Isabella. I need to speak to that woman."

I walked up to her and said, "Hi! Remember me?"

She smiled and nodded.

"I'm looking for Jerry."

"Why? What do you want with him?"

"I want to ask him a few questions, that's all. Do you know where I can find him?"

"I'm not sure ..." she said, looking at me knowingly.

I pulled out my wallet. "Maybe this will help you remember."

I held out a twenty-dollar bill, and she stretched her hand out and left it there while tipping her chin for me to give her more. I pulled out another bill, and she grabbed both in a flash.

"He sometimes sleeps at the underpass near Martin Luther King. Or he may be in one of the deserted buildings in the old section downtown. Be careful, though. He can be a handful," she laughed without joy.

"Okay, thank you," I said as goosebumps crawled along my body.

I climbed back in the car and told Isabella what I'd learned. She said, "Sammy sees her in an old building. I do, too."

I nodded. "The problem is … where's this building located?"

"Why don't we follow some of these people and see where they go?"

"Excellent idea. Let's see who looks promising. Keep an eye on the people who turn left, and I'll watch on the right."

As we sat there, we watched the people coming out of the soup kitchen. Most of them seemed to fade away as if they were invisible, while a few remained near the soup kitchen and eyed Isabella and me, wary of our sitting in the car with no apparent purpose. About 10 minutes later, I pulled out. "Let's head down to the underpass and see if we can find Jerry there."

CHAPTER 48

I was lucky to find an empty parking spot that wasn't too far from the underpass. "Isabella, you stay in the car while I look for Jerry. Keep the car doors locked."

"We're supposed to be a team, Mama."

"We are a team, sweetheart. I don't think it'd be smart for both of us to go. I'll take a quick look around and then come right back."

"Wonder if you don't come back?"

"Don't worry; I'll be back."

I hurried down to the underpass. When I got close enough, I peeked inside to see several people huddled around a small fire burning. Several more people were wrapped up in blankets and lying down, asleep. I stepped inside and called, "Have you seen Jerry?" A few heads turned to look at me and stared without saying anything. I repeated, "Have any of you seen Jerry?"

One of the older men lifted his hand from the blanket wrapped around him and pointed his finger at me. The hair on the back of my neck rose, and goosebumps covered my body. I turned around, and my face ran into the chest of Jerry, who smelled like alcohol and dirty clothes. I recoiled and stepped back away from him.

"Whaddya doing here?" he asked with a maniacal grin. "House hunting?"

I swallowed my fear and said in a firm voice, "I need your help."

"You need *my* help? I ain't got nothing for you, lady."

"It's not for me, Jerry. A young girl has gone missing, and I think Thomas has her. Do you know where he might have taken her?"

He stood looking at me with a funny expression crossing his face. "Another one missing, then?"

I nodded as a thought came to me. "Just like all those young girls years ago. It was the Chief of Police who was responsible for that. Did you kill them?"

At my words, his face grimaced. "That bastard," he said, slurring the words. "He wanted everyone to believe it was me, but it wasn't." He was quiet, lost in thought until he seemed to snap out of his memories. He looked at me anew and took a step toward me. "Why can't you just leave me the fuck alone?"

"Please tell me where Thomas might have taken the young girl, and I'll leave," I pleaded. "I have to find her before it is too late."

"I can't help you," he said, turning away.

"If you find out anything, can you tell Red, and he can tell me?"

Jerry stopped, then turned to face me. "Now, why would I do that?"

"Because you're a good man caught up in something bad. I know you don't want anything to happen to this girl. Jeff always said you were one of the good guys, and I know he wouldn't have said that if it weren't true."

His eyes filled with tears. "He was one of the good guys, too, so you know."

"I do." I took a deep breath. "I'm sorry for what happened to you, Jerry."

He walked away.

I made my way back to the car, downhearted. I had no idea whether Jerry would be of any help or not.

We pulled out and drove toward the old downtown and the large area with empty and neglected buildings tucked in and around. Isabella took one side of the street while I took the other to scout the locations and see if we received a sense of where Tiffany might be. When it started to get dark, we talked with Sammy, and with no new visions coming to any of us, Isabella and I headed home.

CHAPTER 49

T he following day, I was surprised to smell coffee and find the bed empty of Mike. I'd tossed and turned most of the night with anxious thoughts tumbling. When I'd last looked at the clock, it'd been 3:30 a.m. It was barely light out now, and it was still early morning.

A light knock sounded on the bedroom door, and when it opened, Mike stood there fully dressed with a cup of steaming coffee in hand. "Hey, sleepyhead."

"Wow, you're up early."

"We've got a big day ahead working with our new client. We have to get to the place before it opens for business. I thought you might need this before I go."

"Ah, handsome, you know how to win a girl's heart."

He bent and gave me a long, warm kiss. "Remember—no scouting around on your own. Let the police do their work. See you later, sweetheart."

"Later, alligator."

He laughed and left.

I felt that things were coming to a head in the hunt for Tiffany, and I knew all of it wouldn't end well. Despite that, I had no intention of stopping my search for Tiffany. I heard the patter of feet and knew Isabella and Sweet Pea were headed my way. When they entered the room, I patted the empty side of the bed, and both plopped down onto it.

Isabella looked worried but determined. "I'm not going to school today, Mama. I need to find Tiffany now before it's too late."

"Okay, I agree. Let's try holding hands and meditating as we did before. Maybe between the two of us, we can conjure up where Tiffany is, okay?"

She nodded and moved back to rest her head against the headboard so she could relax. I did the same, and we grasped hands and took deep breaths. Soon, the space behind my eyes filled with floating colors. Suddenly, without warning, I felt a searing pain around my heart, and I gasped for air. What was wrong? What was happening? In my mind's eye, I looked down at my burning chest to see that I was a man, and blood was swirling around me. I became frightened. I changed back into myself and tried to scrabble away from the man. He held his hand out to draw me closer, trying to tell me something. Fighting to get away, I jerked out of my trance, but not before I had a chance to see who it was. When I opened my eyes, Isabella's worried eyes were searching mine.

"Mama, who was that man?"

"That was Jerry, and he's hurt. He knows something, too. We need to find him right away. I don't think he was at the underpass, do you?"

"No. It was someplace else."

"Quick! Get dressed, and we'll see if Red is at the construction site. Maybe he can tell us where we can find Jerry."

"Mama?"

"Yes, sweetheart, what's the matter?"

"Look at your hands. Mine too. How come we have blood on our hands?"

"Oh, my God!" Amazing! We had teleported to where Jerry lay. I knew Isabella was powerful as a psychic, having gifts beyond mine. It was obvious that when we worked together, we were mighty powerful—enough to instantly create the energy to transport across space and distance. There was no doubt our spirits had gone to where Jerry lay, and we held the proof that we had. My heart pounded. We needed to find him without delay.

"Get going, kiddo. Hurry!"

As I finished dressing, I heard the squealing brakes of the school bus pull into our driveway. I raced down the stairs and out the front door to tell the driver that Isabella wasn't attending school that day. The door stood open so that I could talk to him, and before he could close it again, Sammy pushed his way forward and off the bus. "I'm coming with you."

I told the driver it was okay, and he backed out of the driveway. "I told my mother I wasth going to be with you today, and she thsaid it was okay."

"I need to call her," I said as I grabbed his jacket and pulled him inside, not happy with him tagging along.

Amazingly, when I spoke with her, she said, "Rosie, you know our children are special, and Sammy won't be deterred. He's determined to find Tiffany, and I feel he's safer with you than going out on his own."

We piled into the car, and I drove to the construction site. Red's truck was there. I told Isabella and Sammy to stay put and hopped out to find Red. He scowled when he saw me approach him.

"Red, you've got to help me!" I yelled while racing closer.

"What is it now?" he responded, scoffing at me.

"I mean it, Red. I need your help."

"What's going on?" he asked, suddenly curious.

"Jerry isn't at the underpass, and I need to find him immediately. Do you know where he could be?"

"Listen, I don't have time for this. I'm not Jerry's keeper. He's a grown man and can do what he wants."

"No, you don't understand. Jerry's hurt, and he needs our help."

"What do you mean? What happened?"

"All I know is we must get to him quickly before it's too late."

"I don't know why, but something tells me you're telling me the truth. Come on, get in the truck. I think I know where Jerry might be."

"I'll have to follow you in my car."

"Okay, hurry."

I drove behind Mike's truck to be right behind him when he drove off the lot. We made a U-turn and headed for the older section of town. It was nearly impossible for me to keep up with Red. He was driving like a wild man. Suddenly, without warning, he slowed down and turned into where a more significant, older deserted building stood. It was a miracle that I hadn't run into the back of his truck.

We all jumped out of the car and raced toward the building, following Red inside. He hollered, "Jerry? Where are you, Jer? Come on out; it's me—Red."

The few people who heard us picked themselves up off the floor and scattered, running away in fear. There was no answer. "Jerry has to be here," Red said.

"He's outback," said Sammy. "I see him out there."

"Me, too," said Isabella. "And he's hurt."

"Stay here, Isabella and Sammy. I don't want you to see this." They didn't argue. They'd seen enough in their visions to know it wouldn't be pretty.

Red raced to the back, and I followed close behind. We rushed out the back door, climbed the stairs, and searched the end of the building for Jerry. The yard was empty of all but broken bottles and scattered litter. "Jerry, where are you?" I called.

Then we heard him. Groaning came from the far side of the building, and we raced forward to find Jerry as I'd seen him in my vision with blood all around him. He had a head wound, but most of the oozing blood came from what appeared to be a stabbing in his abdomen.

"Oh, my God! Call 911," I ordered Red. I went to his side and leaned down close. "What happened, Jerry?"

He reached up and grabbed my hair, pulling me closer. "I found her—the girl you wanted," he panted.

"Where is she?"

"Building off 1st Street." He moaned in pain. "Rosie, need to tell you ...."

"What, Jerry?"

"Chief himself… strangled the girls… made me watch," he panted. When pain attacked him, he must have realized how dire his situation was. He pleaded, "Don't leave me."

Red came to his side, and I moved to hold his head in my lap. I gently pushed the hair off his forehead. "I'm right here, Jerry. I'm not going anywhere."

"Afraid," he whispered, concern on his brow.

"Don't be afraid, Jerry. You have so many people who love you waiting to greet you. Jeff is there, too. He says he wants his best buddy to come and play ball with him. Remember the time when you and he …." My words fell silent, and tears slid down my face as I realized he was gone. I moved and lowered his head to the ground. I bent over him and kissed his forehead. "Thank you for helping us. When we find her, you'll be our hero."

With glistening eyes, Red watched me, never saying a word. I stood and wiped at my tears. "I've got to go."

"Go and find the girl. Make his death count for something. I'll stay with him," ordered Red.

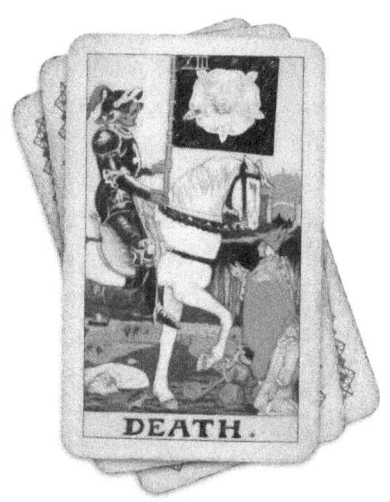

CHAPTER 50

We jumped into the car, and I turned it around and drove toward 1st Street. On the way, I called Roberto at the police station and told him where we were going and why. I asked him to meet us there with no sirens and enough officers to ensure that Thomas didn't escape. I knew the building that Jerry meant, and both Isabella and Sammy intuitively did. They steered me from making a wrong turn and directed me to it. I parked far enough away that we wouldn't tip off Thomas that we were there for Tiffany.

Only after the police surrounded the building did Isabella, Sammy, and I step closer to wait for the okay for us to go inside to retrieve Tiffany. I was nervous about what we'd find inside the building. It seemed to take forever for everyone to get into place, and then the raid began. Guns were raised to the ready by police officers outside the building, waiting to block any escape. Several officers stood by the outside doorways waiting for Roberto to give the word to enter. Finally, Roberto stepped forward with his bullhorn. He thundered, "Thomas and all of you inside, come out of the building with your hands up."

We heard those inside scurrying and shuffling about. Then, all went quiet. Soon, we heard arguing. First, one and then another homeless man stepped outside with their hands raised. But no Thomas and no Tiffany. Roberto raised his bullhorn again. "Before someone gets hurt, c'mon out with your hands up, Thomas."

"I ain't done nothing. I'm not coming out," Thomas yelled.

"Where's the girl, Thomas?"

"She's busy learning her lines. She's going to be a famous movie star."

We looked at each other and shook our heads in disbelief.

"We want the girl, Thomas. Send her out, and no one will get hurt."

"No way. I found her, and she's my movie star," he protested.

"We need to know she's alright. Have Tiffany come to the door for us to see if she's okay."

"She's busy."

I knew that Roberto was trying to figure out what part of the building Tiffany was in so that when they invaded it, they'd know where to find her. Isabella pulled on my sleeve. "Have Roberto ask the two people who came out which room is where the theatre is. That's where Tiffany is right now."

I walked to where Roberto talked with the two people in custody. I overheard him asking them in what part of the building they had last seen Tiffany. They kept repeating that they didn't know, and Roberto was frustrated. I stepped in. "Which room is the theater in?"

Both men perked up at that question. "She's might purty, that one is," said the older man.

"Which room does she perform in?" I pushed.

"The big room downstairs," quickly answered the younger man.

"You mean the old reception area on the first floor?"

"Yup, that's the one," agreed the older man.

"Is that where Tiffany practices her lines, too?"

They nodded. "Thomas says it's the best place to practice. Her voice is loudest there."

Roberto and I eyed each other and stepped away from the two men. Tiffany, on the first floor, was good news. "How many others are in there besides Thomas and Tiffany?" I whispered to Roberto.

"Just them is what these two said," he responded.

Isabella and Sammy walked to where we stood. I asked them. "Those two men said that only Thomas and Tiffany are inside the building. Do you agree?"

They both shook their heads. "There are two others," said Isabella. "One of them is the one who hurt Jerry."

Sammy said, "He acts as Thomas' bodyguard."

Roberto listened, not questioning the validity of what they'd said, and signaled to his Sargent deputy, "There are two other men in there besides the girl and Thomas. Let's give them another five minutes to come out, or we'll go in. Wait for my signal."

The Sargent nodded and relayed the information to those outside the doorways. Then Roberto picked up his bullhorn again. "I'm giving all of you left inside five minutes to come out with your hands held high, or we're coming in. Come out now, and you'll face less trouble."

After a minute or so, one man walked out. He was filthy and looked as if he hadn't eaten in days. My heart went out to him. How could a country as rich as ours have homeless people wandering the streets? I shook my head at myself. I knew better than that. It wasn't that simple, but still.

"It's just me. No more inside," the old man mumbled.

"No, you moron, that's not what you were supposed to say," hollered a voice in anger.

The man's shoulders hunched forward as if protecting himself against the unhappy words that'd been hurled at him, and he shuffled along to where the others in custody waited. As he passed Isabella and Sammy, I watched their faces soften toward the man, and Sammy grasped hold of Isabella's hand and squeezed it. I felt sorry for the man.

Five minutes felt like five hours. Finally, Roberto gave the signal to invade the building. As soon as the men by the doorways clambered inside, Isabella and Sammy raced forward to follow them inside. I hadn't expected them to do that, so I hurried to catch up with them. The building was dark and damp, and its piss and spoiled food odor insulted the senses. Tiffany had most certainly suffered during her stay here. I felt a pang of regret that I'd been so hard on Tiffany when she'd visited our house.

I heard Isabella call out, "Tiffany, where are you?"

I stepped back as Thomas and another man were dragged out of the building by two cops, one on either side.

"Where's Tiffany?" I asked.

The cops shook their heads. "Don't worry, we'll find her."

I immediately went to Isabella and Sammy. "Let's hold hands briefly and see where Tiffany is hiding."

For a full 30 seconds, we stood together with our eyes closed. When we opened them, we looked at each other and said in unison, "Upstairs in the room, farthest back."

We began to climb the stairs. "Tiffany's crying," said Sammy.

"Yes," Isabella and I agreed, feeling some of her pain and shame.

When we walked into the room where Tiffany was hiding, we were surprised to see that it was beautiful in a weird way. The windows had curtains made from torn sheets, and the old mattress on the floor had new colorful blankets brightening the drab paint on the walls. A Beatles poster was nailed onto one wall, and a photo of the Eiffel Tower was on the opposite wall. An odd combination.

The closet door was slightly ajar, and I called, "Tiffany? Are you there? Come on out. You're safe now."

"It's okay. Come on out, Tiff," urged Isabella after a moment.

We heard sobbing from inside and then the shuffling of her feet. The door slowly opened wide. There she stood—tears drying on her face, her hair a mess, her clothes dirty and mussed. We watched her pull herself upright into an arrogant stance. "What took you so long to find me?" she demanded.

There was a second of silence, then we all burst into laughter. I went to Tiffany's side and hugged her. "Tiffany, darling girl, you're never going to change, are you?"

Isabella ran forward. Tiffany's eyes filled, and she reached out to Isabella.

Isabella hugged her. "I'm so glad you're okay."

"Thank you for finding me, Isabella. You too, Sammy." Then, Tiffany straightened, smoothed down her dress, and

279

pushed her long hair behind her. "Are my parents here?" she asked.

"The police have notified them. Your parents should be here any minute now," I answered.

We heard her mother's angry voice outside. "It sounds like they're already here," Tiffany said with a sad smile.

"We'll get out of your way. Are you going to be all right?" I asked.

"Please, don't go," she pleaded.

As loud steps approached, Tiffany took my hand and squeezed it hard. "Don't go! Please!"

Tiffany's mother stood in the doorway. "You? What are YOU doing here?" she asked me. "You and your ward! And who is this? Another ward, I see?"

"They are the ones who found me, Mother. I'm free because of them."

"I think you must be mistaken. You are free because of the police, Tiffany."

"No, Mother. I'm free because of them."

"Enough, Samantha. I said, enough," Tiffany's father warned.

"Daddy, I want you to take me home."

"First, you're going to the hospital so they can check you over, right, Dan?" asked Irene, daring him to defy her."

Tiffany's father lifted his head from holding Tiffany close. He had tears in his eyes. "Sweetheart, you must let them make sure you're all right. I'll stay with you until they are through examining you, then I'll take you home where you belong."

"Okay, Daddy," said Tiffany.

Isabella, Sammy, and I tiptoed from the room, leaving Tiffany to reunite with her parents, who were questioning her. I turned back at the last minute to see Tiffany mouth, "Thank you."

Will wonders never cease? I thought and blew her a kiss before joining Isabella and Sammy.

CHAPTER 51

S ammy called his mother to let him know what'd happened and asked if he could stay for dinner. There was no way I could refuse him or Isabella anything after all they'd experienced.

When we arrived home, I had enough time to make several calls and complete what I had in mind. When I finished, I was pleased. I heard Mike and Brian as they came bursting through the door.

"Are you okay?" Mike asked. "We just heard on the news that a missing girl has been found and is safe. Is that true?"

Brian was right behind Mike. "Are you okay?" he asked, concerned, as he stepped forward to face me. It was like old times for a flash of a second, with the two of them vying for my attention. I smiled at them, my heart full of love for them.

"Is Isabella okay, too?" asked Mike, taking me into his arms.

"Yes, I am," said a tiny voice coming to join us.

Sammy followed with Sweet Pea in his arms. "We all are."

Mike gathered all of us to him, including Brian and Sammy, who laughed at the silliness of it. It was a moment to remember.

Afterward, I turned to Isabella. "I know what you're going to ask me, and the answer is yes," I smiled.

"See, I told you, Sammy," Isabella said.

He laughed. "Okay, then. I want pepperoni on mine." Mike turned to me, shaking his head and smiling. "Why am I not surprised?"

Brian said, "What's going on?"

"It's pizza night, Isabella's favorite dinner."

"Ahh, smart lady," Brian said, tossing her hair.

"Why don't I pour you a glass of wine, Rosie? Brian, grab a beer, and let's hear how things went down," Mike said. "I have a feeling that there's more to come, especially since Roberto told me that Tiffany said there had been other girls who Thomas promised to become a movie star."

"That's upsetting to hear," I said. "That's not good news for sure."

I told them the whole story, including the time I'd met with Jerry at the underpass yesterday that I'd kept from Mike. He looked at me, disbelieving that I'd held back something from him. Then, he tipped his head in resignation that there would be times like that. "Go on," he encouraged.

When I told them what Jerry had said about the Chief of Police killing the girls and making him watch, Mike and

Brian lowered their heads, holding in check their sadness for Jerry's becoming victimized like that.

"That guy was a real prick to make Jerry do that," Brian spouted angrily. "You never get over something like that." We all felt tired and out of sorts when we finished our pizza.

Before Sammy left, I kissed him on the cheek. "You're welcome here anytime, Sammy."

"Thank you." He turned to Isabella and, without any shyness, hugged her and gave her a sweet kiss. "See you tomorrow at school."

I studied the two of them and knew without question that they'd be friends, or maybe more, sharing adventures because of their unique gifts. I sighed. I had to trust that I could keep Isabella safe and we'd be able to enjoy a long time together this lifetime.

That night, I tucked Isabella into bed and lay beside her until we fell asleep. Mike came to get me and carried me to the bed, where I immediately fell back asleep.

The following day, I was the first one awake. I slipped out of bed and raced downstairs to grab the newspaper. I was pleasantly surprised to see my written story splashed across the front page. The headline read, "Former Policeman Hero in Locating Missing Girl. There was a large picture of Jerry smiling in an earlier shot of him in his police uniform. The story said that his heroism had cost him his life and continued to talk about what has become so prevalent today with addiction, homelessness, mental illness, and human trafficking. Purposely, I left out the name of the victim and her family, wanting my article to focus on the hero that Jerry had been.

Staring at the picture of Jerry, my eyes filled, knowing that he, too, had been a victim. He'd joined the police force wanting "to take down the bad guys" and had unwittingly become one due to his sick boss, the Chief of Police, bullying him into witnessing or taking part in all the bad he was creating. That's what abuse of power is all about. It wields and destroys the good.

I crawled back into bed, leaving the newspaper on the kitchen table so everyone else could read it. Last night, we'd discussed with Isabella and Sammy how best to answer the questions bound to be asked of them. Answering "No comment" would allow Tiffany and her family to tell their story how they wanted. We'd have to see how they'd play that out and go from there. Meantime, Isabella and Sammy would meet with the school's counselor. I'd already spoken with the school headmistresses, who agreed with how we would handle things. As I lay there, I heard Brian on the wooden stairs going down, trying to be quiet so as not to disturb us. I smiled. I loved him like the brother I never had, and I was glad he had stayed with us for a while. Mike stirred, and I snuggled against him, grateful for his warmth on a cold winter morning. I was one lucky lady. I had no idea where our relationship would end, but I was willing to enjoy it as it grew.

CHAPTER 52

A fter Mike and Brian were gone and Isabella left for school, I drove to the construction site to meet Romano and Mimi. I'd stopped to buy several more newspapers; I wanted to make sure that Red had a copy for himself.

When I arrived, Romano and Mimi stood by a large truck advertising signs and displays. I got out of my car and waved to them before I searched for Red to hand him his newspaper. As soon as he saw me, he walked to meet me. "Hi, Rosie; what have you got there?"

"Have you seen this morning's newspaper yet?"

"You wrote that, didn't you?" he asked, humbled. I nodded. "It's the least Jerry deserves."

Red, head down, scuffed his right booted foot forward and backward, obviously uncomfortable. "Listen, I owe you an apology. I did try to steal from you with the materials and all. I won't do it again."

I wasn't about to say, 'That's okay,' so I said, "Thank you. What made you change your mind?"

"My mother cried when she read what you wrote. She told me I was breaking her heart and to mend my ways before I ended up like Jerry."

"Wise woman," I said.

"I won't forget what you've done. If you need anything, just let me know."

"Thank you, Red. That means a lot."

Romano and Mimi were flapping their arms to get my attention. They waved me over as two men hooked plastic-covered chains around a large metal sign in the back of the truck. A crane was pulling it skyward, ready to place it in position. Romano and Mimi were grinning from ear to ear, calling out, "Hurry!"

I joined them and looked on as the men twisted the sign for us to see. I sensed Romano and Mimi were watching me closely. When the sign righted itself, I saw the letters Ro and smiled ... Romano's. How nice! When it was fully exposed, my heart stopped. The sign read, "Rosalie's."

"Are you sure?" I turned to them in disbelief. Why wouldn't you want it to read 'Romano's'?"

"I asked Romano the same thing," Mimi said with a smile and a pat on his back.

"This restaurant would never have happened if it weren't for you, Rosie. And you, too, Mimi, of course. But the name Rosalie's has a prettier sound than Romano's."

I felt my face warm with excitement. "Oh, my God! I'm thrilled!" I exclaimed, holding onto Romano and Mimi's hands and dancing around them. "This is so exciting. Thank you so much!"

We watched the men put the sign in place until the end. I took several photos with my cell phone and selfies with the three of us. Then Romano and Mimi left to meet with the decorator, and I went to check in with Roberto at the police station—more paperwork to sign.

When I was nearly done completing the forms, Roberto joined me. "I have interesting news for you, Rosie."

"What is it?"

"You know the body you and Mike found out by the creek?"

"Yeah ..."

"That was another of Thomas' movie stars in the making. He and his henchman have confessed to killing her. Both will be charged with her murder."

"How did the body get out there with the others?"

"They paid Jerry booze and money to get rid of it."

"That doesn't have to become public knowledge, does it?"

"With Jerry dead, we can't prove he buried her there. Since they can't afford a lawyer, Thomas and his henchman will be handed over to a Public Defender. They all have so many cases to handle that whoever takes this one on won't want to take the time to delve into Jerry's part. With their written and recorded confessions of the murder, the Public Defender will hurry through with the murder charges, which will be enough to send them to jail for a very long time."

"Do you know who she is?" I asked.

"Yes, thanks to them, we've identified her. Thomas said, 'She didn't read her lines right.'" Roberto shook his head in disgust. "We're hoping to find out if Thomas is responsible for any other murders. Tiffany seems to think there might be others."

"So much going on here in the shadows. I hope Tiffany can get the help and support she needs through all this," I said.

Roberto raised his eyebrows in surprise, then smiled. "That girl is something else. She tried to order all of us around. Something tells me that with the right help, she will be just fine."

I smiled. "I believe you're right."

CHAPTER 53

I arrived home, spent after a long but satisfying day. I made myself a cup of tea and put my feet up. Sweet Pea came and snuggled next to me on the couch, and I breathed a sigh of relief that all seemed right in the world—for the moment, at least.

I thought of Cal and Virginia. Soon, they'd be living close by. They hoped to be fully moved into their places by the end of next week. I was pleased for them both and happier still to have them be part of our family.

My mind went to Isabella and Sammy. They would be okay with their higher spiritual understanding of what it meant to live in the shadows and survive. Thank God for Sammy's parents. They greatly supported Sammy and now Isabella in accepting the kids' unique psychic gifts.

I thought of how fortunate I was to have my family— Isabella and Mike. How I loved them! They had become such a large part of my life. The phone rang, startling me and breaking into my pleasant thoughts. When I saw it was a conference call from all of my sister-friends, my heart beat with excitement.

"Hi, everyone. What's going on?" I asked.

I heard laughter and hellos. "This is your call, Karen. Take it away," said Susannah in her lawyer voice.

"Yes, Karen, tell us what's happening before I burst!" nudged Nancy.

"I'm so excited. Coyote has asked me to marry him, and I want all of you to be my bride's maids," Karen said.

"Wow! Yes! Of course!" we all answered.

"When is the happy day?" I asked, smiling to myself at how quickly this had come about.

"Saturday, April 11th. Grandmother is preparing two ceremonies that morning, and we'll be married afterward. It'll take place at the Pueblo."

"How exciting!" Nancy exclaimed.

"There's something you should know, though. To participate in the Blessingway ceremony, Grandmother says you'll need a few days to prepare. Do you think you'll be able to take time off?" asked Karen.

We all talked at once. Finally, one by one, we agreed we could.

"Why don't we make it a full sister-friends week? We can stay at my house until the Thursday before the wedding. Then, I'd suggest you book your reservations at the Eldorado Hotel for any time after that," I said.

"Did your parents agree to attend the wedding, Karen?" asked Susannah.

She snorted. "Barely. But don't worry. I won't allow them to take away joy from marrying Coyote."

"Good for you," Nancy said.

We laughed and told each other what was new in our lives. They were impressed that I now had a restaurant named after me, and they promised they'd come for the opening in May. After seven years together, Nancy and her boyfriend were thinking about starting a family, which had all of us whooping with joy. She and her boyfriend still didn't see any need to marry, but maybe that would change down the road. Susannah and Henry were happily considering opening their own law office to serve their law specialties.

After we ended the call, I leaned back against the couch, a pleased smile on my face. I was happy for Karen and Coyote. And it would be so much fun for us girls to have a whole week together where everything would be fantastic. A cloud passed across the sky, darkening the room where I sat. Goosebumps covered my body, and I firmly pushed aside any worries. Wasn't it time for things to go smoothly for a change? Perhaps the rest of the year without any more murders?

I thought about it and then snorted. Who was I kidding?

J.S. PECK

Joan was reared in a family of readers in small-town Elmira, New York. When she was growing up, each Sunday afternoon was a special time when each family member relaxed with a good book.

"It was when I began reading the Nancy Drew series that mysteries intrigued me. To me, the fun of reading mystery books is to become so involved with the story it becomes impossible to put the book down. A good mystery has often caused me to stay up all night to finish it to see whether I can figure out whodunit. For anyone hooked on reading mystery books, there's nothing better than that."

In addition, Joan was raised to be open-minded and understood that we are all connected energetically and can communicate with others who have passed on. She brings that idea into her Death Card series by having the spirit of Rosie's grandmother pop into her life with advice or loving messages. Rosie is portrayed as a psychic, meaning she has visions of what is yet to come.

Joan also writes books under the name Joan S. Peck, and that website is www.JoanSPeck.com.

"I hope you enjoyed reading this book and the entire Death card Series. If so, please help other readers discover it by leaving a review on Amazon.com, Goodreads, or Bookbub. I thank you for your kindness." - Joan

ACKNOWLEDGMENTS

To all of you beautiful readers, I thank you from the bottom of my heart. I hope that you enjoy every chapter and, even more so, find this book difficult to put down. That's what a good mystery is all about.

I was blessed the day I contacted Kelly Martin to be my book cover designer. Thank you, Kelly, for your creativity and artistic talents. I love your work and you!

Thank you, Jake Naylor, for designing my website, laying out my book, and assisting me in many ways with my authoring and marketing. You're a marvel and the best! I love you!

BOOKS BY J.S. PECK

THE DEATH CARD SERIES
- Book 1: *Death on the Strip*
- Book 2: *Death at the Lake*
- Book 3: *Death Returns*
- Book 4: *Death in the Shadows*
- Book 5: *Death on the Run*
- Book 6: *Death Comes Calling*

A HOLIDAY ROMANCE SERIES
- Book 1: *Santa Baby*
- Book 2: *Presents from Heaven*

ROMANTIC MYSTERIES
- *Angels Out of the Dark*
- *The Waiting Room*
- *The Boston Fiasco*

BOOKS BY JOAN S. PECK

- *The Seven Major Chakras – Keeping it Simple*
- *A Simple Approach to Living a Successful Life*
- *What You Need to Know to Live a Spiritual Life*
- *Prime Threat – Shattering the Power of Addiction*